SAM LARSEN
MYSTERIES

SAM LARSEN MYSTERIES

BY JUDY QUAN

ARPress
45 Dan Road Suite 5
Canton MA 02021

Hotline: 1(888) 821-0229
Fax: 1(508) 545-7580

Ordering Information:
Quantity sales. Special discounts are available on quantity purchases by corporations, associations, and others. For details, contact the publisher at the address above.

Printed in the United States of America.

ISBN-13:   Softcover   979-8-89389-770-8
                       eBook   979-8-89389-771-5

Library of Congress Control Number: 2024922594

Table of Contents

Part One: Chasing the Gingerbread Man

Prologue xi

Chapter One 1

Chapter Two 10

Chapter Three 17

Chapter Four 24

Chapter Five 32

Chapter Six 40

Chapter Seven 50

Chapter Eight 56

Chapter Nine 67

Chapter Ten 75

Chapter Eleven 82

Chapter Twelve 91

Chapter Thirteen 97

Chapter Fourteen 105

Chapter Fifteen 113

Chapter Sixteen 121

Chapter Seventeen..127

Chapter Eighteen 135

Part Two: The Aftermath - Honeymoon Homicide

Prologue 147

Chapter One 149

Chapter Two 152

Chapter Three 156

Chapter Four... 160

Chapter Five... 164

Chapter Six 168

Chapter Seven 171

Chapter Eight 173

Chapter Nine 176

Chapter Ten 183

Chapter Eleven... 188

Chapter Twelve 191

Sam Larsen Mysteries

Part One

Chasing the Gingerbread Man

DEDICATION

Many thanks to my husband who tirelessly works with me as my IT guy and morale supporter.

PROLOGUE

There it was again! The spine-chilling, dissonant wail, pitched at an octave that effortlessly penetrated the other storm sounds. How could she describe it? Was it a ghostly screech or the howling of a wounded animal? If so, what species made such an awful noise? Neither description quite fit. Identifying an intermittent scraping, raspy sound in the background was just as elusive.

Atmospheric conditions enveloped the house and created an eerie mood. They could have been plagiarized from a horror film. It was the first night of a new moon, with a palpable darkness, black and velvety, interrupted by flashing zippers of lightning and crescendos of thunder. A steady downpour of icy raindrops, with an occasional outburst of sleet pelted the windows with a strong, staccato force that made Joanne Cavenaugh, the house's sole occupant, fear the aged panes might shatter. She burrowed deeper into her warm cocoon of bedding, pulling the soft, down coverlet over her head.

She craved sleep. She had spent countless nights at her mother's hospital bedside, watching helplessly as the elderly matriarch fought a losing battle with the cancer. The battle had left Joanne emotionally, physically and mentally depleted.

A petite woman, stretching to reach 5 feet tall, and weighing barely 95 pounds, she had shouldered burdens that would exhaust a more robust, younger person. She could not remember the last time her body was free from aches, or when she had slept through the night. She assumed the role of caregiver, refusing to hire a professional with more training and stamina. The chores had not lessened when her mother was admitted to the hospital. Joanne had continued her private care duties there.

Now, she desired only to close her eyes and sink into oblivion of uninterrupted slumber, to replenish stores of energy and optimism long ago depleted. The onslaught of worries, anticipatory grief and sheer physical exertion of trying to meet the obligations of her job as Sheriff's dispatcher, while providing her widowed mother with the care she needed to carry on her war against death, had taken their toll.

For the past eight weeks Joanne had taken leave from work, devoting herself to her mother, as the enemy marched relentlessly forward, robbing the elder woman of her strength, her will to live, her independence and her dignity. Although she clung to life, lying quietly in a hospital bed in a twilight state induced by the morphine drip which coursed through her veins, life as she knew it, and as she had lived it for seven decades, had abandoned her.

Father Peter O'Brian, her parish priest, and Kaye Guinn, a kindly nurse who had been her mother's caregiver during most of her hospital stay, had convinced Joanne to retreat to her mother's house to sleep in a real bed for the night. Her muscles, repeatedly cramped by the lumpy, short hospital cot, now stretched and relaxed. She languished in the warmth and uncrowded space of her bed.

Under other circumstances, Joanne would have welcomed a rainy night, and would have found it relaxing. Tonight, however, the rain created an inexplicable uneasiness and fear which induced insomnia instead. The wind, while not excessive in velocity, attacked the icy precipitation with intermittent gusts, spinning it into mini torrents, which whipped against the house with an eerie rhythm. It ripped at the forlorn branches of the ancient oak tree outside her bedroom window.

The high pitched grating sound, like fingernails scraping against a chalkboard, interspersed the symphony of eerie storm sounds with increasing frequency. As the tiny hairs on the back of her neck stood on end, she hypothesized about its origin. It was unlike any natural sound that she had ever heard. To call it supernatural, however, would be exaggerating. Perhaps the wind had fractured a branch, and that was what scraped against the house. She willed herself to ignore the sound, but it defied all of her attempts to shut it out. The pitch isolated it from the other storm sounds, and magnified it to an unbearable level. Her keen sense of hearing became her enemy, interfering with her body's intense need for rest, and her mind's quest for temporary oblivion.

Reluctantly Joanne emerged from her soft, warm haven of bedding. She slipped her feet into quilted slippers, then shrugged her arms into a flannel robe. She thought, perhaps if she warmed a cup of milk and sat in the kitchen for a while, the storm would abate, taking the unbearable, raspy- scraping- wailing with it.

Hannah, her mother, would have marched outside and stripped the offending branch from the tree, rendering it incapable of continuing its irritating concerto. But Joanne possessed neither her mother's courage nor decisiveness.

Joanne's father had died before she was born. Hannah had raised Joanne alone, never once complaining that life as a single mother was difficult and lonely. Joanne was often puzzled that her mother had never remarried or seriously dated another man. Hannah had been attractive, witty and warm hearted. Many men would have welcomed such a woman into their life. Joanne admired her mother's loyalty to her father's memory, but often wished that she had a father substitute, and her mother had found romantic companionship. Father O'Brian had remained a loyal friend to both mother and daughter, and had provided male guidance in his gentle, caring manner. But, Joanne was sure that a celibate companion, while better than loneliness, hardly compared to the fulfillment her mother could have enjoyed had she remarried.

Now, as Joanne waited for her milk to warm, she mused about the irony of her life. Her mother, never one to be daunted by a challenge, had met hers head-on, without reservation. She had never let widowhood slow her down. A well-educated woman for her generation, she had worked as a bookkeeper at a local construction firm for Joanne's entire life. Joanne, however, was an introvert, and despite her mother's attempts to instill assertiveness and self-confidence in her, had matured into a shy, reticent adult, who shunned social contact. Her coworkers at the sheriff's office were her friends, but she confined her contacts with them to working hours and obligatory social events.

Now in her fifties, with the death of her only relative and companion imminent, she resigned herself to living a solitary life. Yet she did not find this prospect disturbing. She enjoyed her own company. While her mother had flourished in the business world once thought to be a man's domain, Joanne had excelled in the domestic realm. The exquisite crafts and needlework projects which adorned their home were the fruits of many hours of happy solitude spent creating beauty, while shutting out a world which she found overwhelming. Her work as a law enforcement dispatcher only reinforced her belief that the world was an ugly, frightening place, and one which she chose to avoid.

The screeching of the persistent sound, much like the noxious beating of the heart in Edgar Allen Poe's fiction, now amplified and seemed to shift its location, following her from room to room. It agitated Joanne as she sat in the cozy kitchen, sipping her mug of hot milk. Was it her imagination that made its volume and frequency seem to increase? Was her sleep-deprived mind distorting reality? She hoped that it was her imagination, but the sound seemed to follow her to the kitchen, on the opposite side of the house from her bedroom, where she first heard it. No trees grew near the kitchen. Perhaps her theory about its origin was wrong. But if it was not caused by a broken limb scraping the house, what could it be? She was sure her exhaustion both created and exacerbated the irritation. But she was equally sure that she would not achieve the sleep she coveted until the sound stopped.

She shivered. With trepidation and fear tagging along as unwelcome companions, she donned an overcoat, slipped her mother's overshoes over her slippers, and she unlocked the kitchen door. As she stepped outside into the piercing cold of the wet, windy night, she grabbed the emergency flashlight from its place on the windowsill. Stepping gingerly through the yard, attempting to avoid the pools of slippery mud and puddles of rain water, Joanne flicked the flashlight on and waited for its light to pierce a narrow pathway through the intense darkness. She uttered and expletive as she realized the batteries had died. Frustrated and frightened by the darkness, with nothing to illuminate it, she trudged on, attempting to navigate by groping the house's external surface. She nearly lost her footing more than once, but dug her fingers into the siding to regain her balance.

She rounded the corner, arriving at the location outside her bedroom where she was certain the sound had originated, then stopped in her tracks and gasped. The massive old tree whose branches she suspected of causing the sound, stood stalwart against the onslaught of the wind, its branches intact. No fractured or loose branches brushed the house or bobbed in the wind. They had been neatly trimmed months earlier by the yard crew her mother hired to manicure the lawn and tree. Branches near the house had been pruned to avoid contact with it.

More annoyed than puzzled, Joanne paused, and then turned to retrace her steps. But her breath was suddenly stolen by an unseen band which coiled around her neck. Gasping for breath, she flailed her hands in midair, and then lifted one hand to claw at the band, desperate to remove it from her throat. Her strength and control of her bodily functions deteriorated rapidly as oxygen deprivation closed in, and she dropped the useless flashlight in the mud. The smell of wet leather from the gloved hand which batted her hand away barely registered in her panicked mind. Thoughts tumbled on top of each other, with past memories and present sensations merging into a confusing, terrifying kaleidoscope of images.

Then all images ceased, and thoughts were replaced by blackness. Stillness prevailed, as Joanne slipped into the realm of afterlife which Father O'Brian had often addressed in his Sunday sermons. Her limp, lifeless body, suspended only by the band around her throat and the brutal hands which held it, swayed slightly in midair. Rubber bands replaced the muscles in her legs. She was transformed into a human rag doll, arms drooping at her sides, neck and head falling forward onto her chest. Life, as a fleeting mist, escaped, vaporizing into a mysterious realm from which no one ever returned. Obeying Nature's command, her body slipped to the ground.

Chapter One

My dreams faded in and out of focus, alternating between realistic encounters with people who intersected my life, and a cast of surrealistic science-fiction characters. Black and white, interspersed with vivid color, with an occasional intrusion of sound like a violent thunderstorm, formed the backdrop for these sleep dramas. Somewhere between scene changes, I reached through a fog to slap at the alarm clock, to silence its buzzing. But as I groped for the snooze button for the third time, my drowsy mind rallied to a semi-awake stage when I realized the clock was not alarming. My pager was buzzing. A bit old school, with the advent of the cell phone, I still used a pager to triage my calls and avoid answering the phone when I was busy or didn't want to be disturbed. The pager was used for only the most urgent calls; my own 9-1-1 system. The realization jolted me awake. A bolus of adrenaline shot through my body, dashing my face with a splash of reality. Glowing numbers on the clock peered at me through the darkness. It was 4:30 a.m.

My alert system dictated that anyone who urgently needed to reach me start by a page, then ring me up on the phone, so I knew to answer it right away. When the pager alert was followed by the phone call, I fumbled to answer the phone, missed the call, and it rolled to voice mail. My office number appeared. I knew right away that something serious had happened. As lead detective of the homicide division of the County Sheriff's Department, I knew the news I was about to receive would not be pleasant. I dialed the station. When my boss, Chief Sutton, answered the call, I knew the news was going to be very bad. Chief was never awake at such an early hour, and he never answered the office phone, himself.

"Sam", Chief barked, his voice uncharacteristically harsh. "Get yourself together and don't waste any time making yourself pretty."

A city patrol officer, answering a 9-11 call from an orderly at County Hospital, had discovered the partially nude body of our own long-time emergency dispatcher, Joanne Cavenaugh, lying face down in a pool of muddy water in a vest- pocket greenbelt area next to the Emergency Room entrance. The orderly, who was coming to work early, had noticed something unusual in the park, and had waded through the mud to investigate.

Chief shared the scant preliminary details with me as I tucked the phone under my chin, pulled jeans and sweatshirt from my dresser, then started the shower. I hung up, then quickly lathered and rinsed, letting the warm water trickle down my face and body. Mornings like these convinced me that I had made the right decision a year ago, when I had cut my shoulder length hair to a short bob. I could dry it quickly and be out the door in less than twenty minutes. I was blessed with a low upkeep face, too. Although my pale complexion reflected my northern European heritage, I seldom needed much make-up to brighten the ivory-pink skin. A generous sprinkling of freckles across the bridge of my nose, which had not faded as I left my twenties, gave me a youthful look that belied my years of investigative experience. My cheeks usually carried enough color to keep me from looking pale. After whipping the minty paste on my toothbrush into a frothy scrub for my teeth, I rinsed, flicked on a touch of mascara and lightly tinted lip gloss, touched a bit of moisturizer on my face, and my no nonsense beauty routine was complete. I slipped into my jeans and was on my way to the crime scene in record time. I had no way of knowing how drastically this case would change my life in a very short period of time. But, I was about to find out.

Yellow crime scene tape already cordoned off the area by the time I arrived. Detective Robert Rosini had arrived ahead of me, a fact that didn't elicit warm thoughts or confidence. I approached the scene and could see that he had carelessly waded into the inner parameters of the scene, and now stood next to the victim's body. Although we logged every person who entered a crime scene so that we could exclude our team members' forensic contributions from external evidence, the condition of the crime scene guaranteed that any intrusion on the scene was sure to obscure pertinent evidence. The crime scene photographer had not yet arrived. The forensics team parked its van next to mine as we arrived simultaneously. So, it was doubtful that any foot prints or other evidence had been preserved before our arrival.

I was sure Rosini had contaminated evidence with his carelessness. His footprints would be commingled with the other prints in the mud. Although the rain had slowed to an occasional drizzle, footprints near the body would be difficult to cast. Water puddled in many of the crevices, and the ground looked like trampled mud in a cattle pen. Not only had our own detective added his prints to the chaotic tracks, but the frightened orderly who found the body had stepped close to it to see if she was alive, before running to call for help. The only person on scene who had not violated the integrity of the evidence was the patrol officer who had strung the yellow tape.

Mistakes like these had cost Rosini the promotion to head of homicide detectives two years earlier. He had never forgiven me for getting that promotion instead, and would never understand that he had robbed himself of that opportunity. He continued to blame me, and insinuated that I had somehow earned the promotion on my back, instead of on my feet, as a competent, hard-working cop. He eyed every superior officer who had any input into the decision as my consort, even though I had been happily involved with State District Judge, Nathaniel Beck for over three years, and we were planning to marry in a few months.

False modesty aside, I admit that I am attractive in an "Ivory Soap," girl-next-door sort of way. I look more wholesome and cute than glamorous, with strawberry blonde hair that fades in winter to a subtle, dark blonde, and lightens to a pale champagne in summer. I'm neither petite nor voluptuous. I keep my weight in check and muscle mass respectable by jogging three times a week, and lifting weights. I was far from the seductive vixen image that Rosini had tried to promote. My martial arts and weapons skills were developed during my early years as a female cop in a male dominated environment, where I needed to be more competent that the men, in order to receive equal respect. Having trained under one of the best investigators in a large, metropolitan police force in Texas, I knew that my detective skills, not my sex, had been the basis for my promotion. Rosini began his campaign to discredit me as his equal starting my first day on the job, but that had eventually discredited him instead.

Rosini was a study in contrast. His outward appearance camouflaged smoldering inner conflicts. A short, muscular man, he had been blessed with a face that met all of the qualifications for being attractive in a rugged, well-proportioned way. In his younger years he must have been considered quite handsome. He retained some of the handsome exterior as he aged, but the years had not been kind to him. He had aged beyond his years, and the roadmap of his features disclosed several detours into bitter discontent. Now in his late forties, his face bore the etchings of too many hours in the sun, and too much indulgence in alcohol and nicotine.

He had been married for a few years while still in his thirties, but that relationship had been volatile, and there had been unconfirmed rumors of domestic violence. His wife divorced him and left the State. I had heard gossip that she was afraid to stay nearby, fearing Rosini would abuse his power as an officer of the law, to harass her or make her life hell in subtle ways that couldn't be proven. According to my sources, he had given her a sample of what he was capable of before she left, but nobody could confirm it, and Rosini had never been held accountable for it. My gut reaction to that report was to believe it, not based on something tangible, but on what I sensed lurked beneath his facade of civility.

The Department grapevine churned out a number of reports of romantic entanglements between Rosini and unsuspecting females over the ensuing years, but he had been unable or unwilling to sustain a long-term relationship with any of them. His "relationships" rarely survived longer than a week or two, before the disillusioned young women broke it off, putting as much distance between themselves and Rosini as possible.

Rosini still retained a number of physically attractive features, with a lavish headful of dark, wavy hair, intertwined with gray, and eyes so dark brown that one had to look very closely to see his pupils. I usually detected a steely coldness in those eyes when I looked at him. I couldn't decide if that coldness reflected his personal animosity towards me, or if it mirrored his inner character. I had seldom seen him smile, but had observed an occasional flash of straight white teeth, framed by full, sensuous lips when he spoke to others. How quickly those sensuous lips transformed into a smirk or twisted into a snarl when he spoke to me. He had seemed to smile most often when visiting with Joanne Cavenaugh, our dispatcher, while enjoying the homemade baked goods she often brought to share with her co-workers.

Joanne Cavenaugh had been a quiet, gentle woman, who seemed to bring out a softer, gentler side of Rosini, that we seldom saw otherwise. Although Joanne was childless, she acted a maternally towards Rosini, and he responded by acting protective and chivalrous towards her. I had heard through the department grapevine that Rosini had lost his own mother in a tragic accident when he was a teenager. Some who knew him claimed that he blamed himself for the accident, and had never fully recovered from his loss, growing more bitter with each passing year. Joanne seemed to fill part of the void left by his loss.

My own heart softened a bit as I realized how Joanne's death must be torturing him. I wondered if he should be pulled off the case. Perhaps his grief had caused him to be more careless than usual in his handling of the crime scene. I knew from previous interactions with him, though, that I would have a major battle on my hands if I tried to remove him from the case against his will. I would have to watch his actions to see if he further endangered the investigation, or risk diverting a substantial amount of time, effort and concentration away from the investigation to pursue his removal.

During more magnanimous moments, I conceded to myself that Rosini was not really a bad sort of person. We just saw life from opposing vantage-points. But on more realistic moments, such as the Cavenaugh crime scene, I felt less than magnanimous, and admitted to myself that I despised Rosini as much as he obviously despised me. I had no respect for him - either personally or professionally, and considered him to be a blemish on the countenance of the County Sheriff's department.

At best, he was mediocre as a cop. He had survived professionally by joining the department when the population of the county was very small, with very little crime. The cases he handled during his first decade as a deputy had been uncomplicated and usually minor. He formed a few alliances with people who rose in the ranks at the Department, and they offered him enough support to allow him to remain employed, even though they realized he lacked investigative skills to justify a promotion. As the complexity and number of cases grew, he did not grow to meet the new demands, so he resorted to defensive, often obnoxious behavior to mask his lack of ability and insecurity. He was especially inept in handling forensic evidence, and his glaring inadequacies did not go unnoticed by his superiors. He had seniority over me at the department, having served for nearly eighteen years. But, his deficient investigative skills stunted his professional stature, and negated any benefits that seniority might have offered him.

Although I was a newcomer to this area, I was not inexperienced. In addition to serving as an officer for five years on the police force in Texas before moving to the Midwest six years earlier, and had earned a college degree in criminal justice with a minor in psychology, prior to joining the Texas police academy.

As the forensics team and I approached the body, Rosini glanced in my direction, then looked down at his feet. His expression was hard to read. Part of it resembled my kid brother's when he knew he had done something wrong, but couldn't admit it. But there was more to it, a certain defiance, almost like he was proud he had messed up the crime scene, and dared me to say something about it. If he had been my kid brother, I would have delivered a scolding and sent him to his room. Instead, I had to salvage what I could of the evidence, and hope we could still find the killer with clues that had not been disturbed. I would write-up Rosini for his carelessness later. If we hoped to find Joanne's killer, we needed to focus on more pressing matters at the moment.

The forensic team members were casting footprints, photographing every angle of the scene and bagging every piece of material near the scene when the Medical Examiner, Dr. Karl Pendleton arrived. Karl was a friend of mine, and a very skilled forensic pathologist. Having him working the case gave me a glimmer of optimism about our ability to solve it. He and I had worked on many homicides together over the years, and I always marveled at his attention to detail and his analytical genius. He had been responsible for piecing together many major pieces of the homicide puzzle on some of my most difficult cases, using his keen observation skills and tenacity to find the answers. I was genuinely relieved and encouraged by his arrival.

"Doc, you are a sight for sore eyes," I smiled and called out to him. He grunted a response. I knew he wasn't a morning person. The dark circles ringing his eyes told me he had worked very late the night before. I knew once he started working the crime scene his eyes would take in every detail, his marvelous mind would photograph and archive each one of them. Given the opportunity to drink a few strong cups of coffee, his personality would also revive and the nice, but eccentric guy that was hidden at the moment, would emerge. He glanced at the scene, and when he saw Rosini standing near the body, he asked, "What in hell is *he* doing here?" Doc had seen more of Rosini's incompetence than I had over the years, and his opinion of Rossini was even more negative than mine. I shrugged and shook my head to indicate it hadn't been my idea. He plodded through the mud, lost in his own thoughts, until he reached the yellow tape. Then, like a seasoned battlefield General, he took charge of the scene.

After a brief pause, the forensic team continued its evidence gathering. Everyone, except for Rosini, nodded a greeting in Doc's direction. Prints had been cast with quick-drying impression material; the victim's hands had been covered with bags to preserve evidence that might lurk beneath her fingernails. After the entire area had been painstakingly photographed, it was ready for Doc's inspection. He observed the victim's dorsal side with great care , then he and one of the forensic team gently turned the body over, so he could inspect the front.

I barely stifled a gasp, and I noticed that Rosini flinched involuntarily. The victim's face was a dark, bluish color. Her tongue protruded and was swollen. Her lifeless, blood stained eyes stared out from open lids. An angry red welt encircled her neck. She had been strangled with some sort of rope or band, with such force that a portion of the throat wound was lacerated. The band had been removed, however, and was nowhere in the immediate area. I surmised that she had probably struggled against the material, since fragments of flesh had separated from the welt and hung in tattered strips at her throat. I felt Rosini's eyes drill into me as an involuntary wave of nausea collided with my stomach and my scalp contracted into a thousand tingling shockwaves.

I was a time traveler on the deja vu express, traveling backwards to a similar crime scene in Texas, eight years ago. The tattered flesh on that victim's throat had never been avenged; and there had been no justice. Dust gathered on the cold case file as it kept its place among other frustrating unsolved murders. God help us! Was the same dark, psychotic mind now prowling our County streets and roadways, preying on Midwestern innocents?

The mood was exceptionally solemn, and the forensics crew silent as Doc finished his preliminary exam at the site, and Joanne's body was gently zipped into a body bag, loaded onto a gurney, then into the van for transport to the morgue. Each team member finished his work and walked silently to individual vehicles. We all knew the routine. We would gather at the main conference room for debriefing and strategizing by early afternoon. Determination to solve this crime was written across each face.

Chapter Two

Driving back to the office, I mused about how little I knew about the victim. She had been a fixture at the department for many years before I joined it. We all interacted with her on a daily basis, and could count on her stability and calm manner, even during the most emotionally charged incidents. I had briefly encountered her while still living in Texas, during my trips to Iowa to investigate the murder so ironically similar to her own. I had been impressed even then by her quiet, warm nature but knew little else about her. She had not impressed me as the woman most likely to fall victim to a brutal murderer. I was saddened a bit by the knowledge that I would really only know this woman posthumously, and that I had perhaps missed an opportunity to enjoy a friendship with her.

News of Joanne's death had already rippled through the Sheriff Department headquarters before I arrived. Her personnel file had been pulled for my, and Janis Jacobs, the personnel director brought it to me in person. I was aware that Joanne had not been on duty for a while, and vaguely knew that a family member was ill. But I knew little else about her personal life, or the reason for her absence. I discovered that Joanne's mother was her only kin, and that she was so ill she might not understand that her daughter was dead.

The remainder of her personnel file and my discussion with the director yielded very little information, except for Joanne's home address. She had listed her mother and her priest as emergency contacts, and had given the priest as a personal reference when she applied for the dispatcher's job eighteen years ago. Her job performance had been consistently satisfactory, and she had never been reprimanded or written up for negative performance or attendance. During the course of her mother's illness she had been tardy a few times, but her supervisor had given her grace.

Stifling the urge to procrastinate, as I sometimes did when faced with an unpleasant task, I left the meeting with the personnel director and drove to County Hospital to meet Joanne's mother. I nearly collided with Father O'Brian as I stepped off the elevator. His wrinkled face wore a mask of pale distress. I introduced myself and explained why I had come. He nodded, looking at me, while avoiding my eyes. A silvery drop of moisture glistened in the corner of his eyes. Dried, salty streaks on his cheeks broadcast to the attentive observer that he had been weeping. He told me he had already heard about Joanne's death, then quietly led the way to Hannah's room. We kept the lights off, allowing only the small amount of sunlight peering through the curtains of the single, small window. Father O'Brien explained that sound and light disturbed his friend, and he wanted to keep her as comfortable as possible. The doctors expected her to live only a day or two longer. She seldom ascended from her valley of oblivion to a level of consciousness. Mercifully, the drugs were successful in controlling the gnawing pain of advanced cancer.

The priest led me to the window and pointed outside. The view from the window faced the alley. Next to the alley was the greenbelt where Joanne's body had been found. He was in Hannah's room when the investigation team had arrived on the crime scene, and had found out about Joanne's death by watching us zip her body into the body bag.

Father O'Brian clutched prayer beads close to his heart with one hand, while silently making the cross with his other hand. He stared vacantly out the window, slipping away to a place where I could not follow.

"Father, I'm sorry, but you know I have to ask you some questions," I whispered. I tried to be as gentle as possible, but I still had to do my job. He shook his head slightly, as if to clear his mind, and looked at me, blue-gray eyes reddened, but clear.

"Yes, of course. But, please let's go outside in the hall," he whispered. "The nurses tell me that she can hear, even if she is under," he motioned to the woman in the bed.

I had not known Hannah Cavenaugh before her illness. Now her appearance resembled pictures I had seen of Hitler's concentration camp victims. Translucent, yellowish skin stretched over her tiny skeleton, without any fat to cushion it. The priest stopped by her bedside as we made our way to the door, to adjust the oversized terrycloth turban covering her hairless scalp. "I think losing her hair traumatized her more than any other part of her treatment," he said, more to himself than to me. Then, his voice trailed away, even less audible than before. I followed his gaze and noticed that Hannah didn't seem to be breathing. I instinctively held my breath. So did the priest. Then after a very long pause, she gasped, took two or three quick gasps and stopped again. Having worked my way through college as an emergency medical technician at a Texas ambulance service, I recognized the Cheyne-Stokes breathing pattern, and realized death was not far away.

Hannah's face distorted momentarily, and I wondered if she was in pain. "Henry, Henry." she mewed faintly. Who the heck was Henry? I wondered. Perhaps I had read her lips incorrectly.

The priest quickly bent over her, gently stroking her forehead. "I'm here, my love," he whispered, in a voice I barely recognized. I blinked in surprise as he kissed her forehead, then her tiny, bony hand. She relaxed and drifted back into her sleepy daze.

I waited until we stepped into the hall to ask the priest about the scene I had just witnessed. "Who is Henry?" I asked.

"Someone she once loved very much," he said. A slight smile touched his lips, and his eyes stared into another dimension again.

"Do you know where I can find Henry?"

"He's been gone for many years, so no, you can't find him."

"Father O'Brian, do you always so intimately comfort your parishioners?" Even as I asked the question, I regretted having to be so blunt.

"I am whoever she needs me to be. I've been her friend since she came here to Iowa. I've watched her daughter, Joanne grow up. If I can bring her comfort on her death bed by being Henry, then I shall be Henry." His jaw transformed into a hard line of determination, and he raised the angle of his chin slightly, to emphasize his resolve as he answered, almost defiantly. Then his face softened again to the appearance I recognized.

I continued my dialogue, "Forgive me for prying, Father, but I 'm trying to piece together a puzzle which will help me understand her life and her daughter's life. Understanding their backgrounds might help me bring Joanne's killer to justice. I am going to have to ask more questions that you might not like, but I need for you to answer them. I wouldn't ask them if it wasn't important. I promise, I won't ask anything out of idle curiosity."

He smiled, and then said, "I'm the one who asks your forgiveness, my child. I would like to pass off my behavior as fatigue, but I confess that my heart is breaking. I won't allow anyone to harm her or her reputation, in life or in death. Please, allow me to help in any way I can."

I found his last dissertation a bit jumbled and rambling. Why would anyone want to harm Hannah's reputation? I had no intention of doing so. Unless she had a darker, secret past that would come to light as I dug around to find pertinent information during my investigation. If that was the case, the priest's statements were almost a threat.

"Were you here all night, Father?" I asked.

"Yes, since I am officially retired, and do not draw a salary from the church, they allow me freedom to spend as much time as a situation requires. Father Hansen tends to the daily needs of the parish. I have spent most of my time in that hospital room since Hannah became terminal. Until last night, her daughter spent most of her time here, also. Joanne slept on a cot in the room most nights. I sent her home last night to sleep in a full sized bed, and stayed here on the cot in her place."

"Did you see anything outside the window during the night that was out of the ordinary?" My interrogation continued.

"No, I slept most of the night. I woke up around 4:30 or so in the morning when the red flashing lights and sirens pulled into the alley. I've heard so many ambulances, yet somehow I knew this was different. At first I didn't know it was Joanne...." His voice trailed off, and he bowed his head. Once again, he was in a place where I could not go.

"Father, did Joanne have any enemies? Do you know why anyone would want to kill her?"

"No, no, no! She was the most innocent and gentle person I know…knew. She was a devoted daughter, loving friend. She was a timid sort, not a real social butterfly. But she cared about people. She helped anyone who needed help. I was so proud of her. You know, for about ten years she was a Nun. But, she reached a point where she didn't feel God had called her to the convent, so she left it." She hated the ugliness she came in contact with as a dispatcher. She told me she felt violated by the crimes that touched her through her job, but she wanted to bloom where she was planted. She felt she was doing her mission there, even among the pain and ugliness."

I was momentarily surprised by the passion with which he answered my questions about Joanne. I decided to change the subject. "I need to notify next of kin.."

He answered before I could finish my question. "She has none. They had only each other. She was an only child, and Hannah's parents died many years ago. They weren't close. I will be making all of the arrangements for their funerals and burials."

There was finality to his last statement that doubled as a dismissal. I had no more pressing questions, but told the priest that I might have more questions later. As an afterthought, he reached into his pocket and produced a key. "Joanne gave me this key to their house, so I could look in on things, water her plants, and check the mail, when she stayed here at the hospital. Maybe you will need to go in there for something. There might be some kind of information there that I can't think of right now. I truly want you to catch who killed her. I'm sorry I can't be of more help." He squeezed my hand as he placed the key in it and turned to go back into Hannah's room.

"Wait, Father, one more question."

He turned slightly to face me.

"Do you know where Joanne's car is? We have searched the hospital parking garage and can't find it."

"All I know is she drove here and was to drive home. It doesn't look like she made it home, though, does it?"

I watched the aged priest quietly open the door and slip into the presence of his beloved friend. I had an unsettled feeling that he hadn't told me everything. He had told me the truth, but not the whole truth. I wondered what was he hiding, and why.

I glanced at my watch. If I hurried back to the station, I would only be 30 minutes late for the meeting with the other detectives and officers assigned to this case.

Chapter Three

I was out of breath as I rushed into the conference room. I saved time by not waiting for the ancient, unreliable elevator and ran up three flights of stairs. "Y'all, thanks for waiting. Sorry I'm a bit late." I offered no further explanation, and none of the detectives, except Rosini, seemed to have any problem with it. I noticed he smirked at the "y'all", but I didn't care. I had worked hard to neutralize a very strong southern accent after moving here, but couldn't bring myself to give up that one last remnant of my Texas roots.

I wondered what had possessed the Chief when he assigned Rosini to this case. As it had for at least a dozen times throughout the morning, the mere thought of Chief making that duty assignment, angered me. It welled up inside me like acid reflux after a spicy meal. I choked back the sensation, and dismissed the fury that threatened to build, choosing to postpone my indignant objections until a more appropriate time.

I reviewed the assignment roster for the case. I had subconsciously chosen team members who had at least one positive quality to offset Rosini's negative qualities.

George Simmons, a young, energetic five year patrol officer, had been temporarily loaned to me to work on the case. He had demonstrated maturity, initiative, good judgment, and investigative talent on a couple of my cases in the past. He also took nothing for granted, left ego at home, and was a team player. I knew I would need someone like George on our team, because Rosini had already proven that his ego was not on vacation, and he had no intention of being a team player.

Patrick Addison, a veteran detective, who was two years from retirement, added another cornerstone of stability to our team. He wasn't especially energetic or ambitious, but he took his duties seriously, and had not adopted a short-timer's attitude like some other officers who were near retirement. He had nothing to prove and just wanted to do a good job.

Paul Sorenson, the City patrol officer who had responded to the 9-1-1 call, and discovered Joanne's body, was also recruited for the team. I was impressed by his cautious and professional approach at the crime scene, and wanted to draw on all of his observations from the scene.

The only loose cannon on the team was Rosini. Otherwise, we had a solid, stable group of professionals. I still believed that the team would be better off without Rosini, but I wanted to hit the trail of evidence before it grew cold. That meant I had to decide at least temporarily, not to spend a lot of time and energy on removing Rosini from the case. I still could not fathom why Chief Sutton assigned him in the first place. Life would be a lot easier if he had not. I doubly resented the fact that he had not consulted me before putting Rosini on the team. I had carte blanche to pick all other team members, yet he had assigned Rosini before I was given a chance to object. I would wait and see, and act later to remove Rosini if it became necessary. I hoped he would be more dedicated, professional and cooperative on this investigation than on his other cases, since the victim had been his friend.

"O.K., let's see what we have so far." I switched on a digital recorder and picked up a marker for the white board. Rosini rolled his eyes. He didn't need to say that he thought I acted too "big city", with my investigative methods. He had complained long and loudly about it before. But, my methods had been too successful to argue with, and I had no intention of changing them.

"Has the lab given us anything yet?" I asked. Simmons and Sorenson answered in unison. I knew some of the evidence would take several days for forensics to process, but hoped they had something for a starting point. Nobody had heard from them. I volunteered to go by the lab, myself on my way out to Joanne's house after the meeting.

"Rosini, I need for you and George to talk to the hospital orderly who found the body." No argument. Good. I didn't think Rosini could find fault with the assignment, but I never knew what was going to set him off. The orderly was an important witness, and I didn't think Rosini could mess up an interview with him, especially if I sent George with him. I didn't trust Rosini to go alone, and hoped he would think I was sending George because the orderly was important enough to warrant two detectives. "While you are at the hospital, please split up and talk to all of the ER staff, security guards, and find out which paramedics and private ambulances brought in patients to ER last night. I'd like for the two of you to interview all of them, too."

I assigned Pat and Paul to interview Joanne's coworkers.

Before he left for the hospital, I asked Rosini to stay behind so I could question what he knew about Joanne. As one of her personal friends, I wanted to know if there were other friends, enemies or lovers that we should know about. When I asked, Rosini shot me a poisoned look. He replied curtly, "No enemies. No lovers. Everyone was her friend. There are some women who know how to be women, if you know what I mean," he smirked, then continued, "No, I guess you don't." I ignored his sidebars, so he continued, but added nothing to the information I had already learned from my earlier conversation with Father O'Brian.

Rosini added his own commentary without being asked. "I think the old priest is a little weird, if you ask me," he piped in. "Nothing definite, but I think the old pervert had a thing for Joanne's mother. I want to talk to him. I guarantee I can get it out of him, if he did."

I vetoed his plans, and told him, "I've already talked to Father O'Brian this morning, and if there is any follow-up to do, I'll do it," I emphasized that further interrogation of the priest was not open to debate. I knew Chief would back me 100% on this point, and so did Rosini. He opened his mouth to argue with me, but shut it again without comment. I wasn't sure if his closed mouth meant he was going to ignore my decision, and go ahead with interrogating the priest anyway, or if he accepted it. I hated having a detective on the team who was so volatile and unpredictable!

The phone rang just then, and I breathed a silent prayer of thanks for the reprieve. It was Doc. He had finished the gross part of the autopsy, but wouldn't have lab reports back for several days. He confirmed cause of death was strangulation. That was no surprise. The details he had dictated for his report also confirmed that the murder had been every bit as brutal as it had looked at the crime scene.

Doc had clipped her fingernails and sent them to the lab for further examination as well, but wasn't optimistic about any evidence there, either. Her nails had appeared freshly cleaned, either by the victim or the murderer. Joanne had not been killed at the site where her body had been discovered. She had been killed elsewhere, and then moved to that location, a deliberate, pre-mediated move, apparently calculated to deliver a message. But what was the message, and to whom was it directed? Her body had been deposited within clear view of her mother's hospital room, where the aged priest kept his vigil.

Our first task was to figure out where Joanne was murdered. Then forensics would have to go over that scene for evidence, as they had the scene where the body was dumped. An APB for Joanne's car had already circulated among all County officers and police departments in the county. Much of the County was rural, with numerous out-of-the-way wooded areas which could conceal a car, murder evidence, or the murderer. The river and its tributaries provided ample opportunity for evidence to be discarded into a watery grave, never to be found, one that was taken advantage of entirely too often. I wondered how many fishermen's snags encountered in the river were actually pieces of evidence from old crimes.

Doc had also determined from the lividity, that the body had been moved shortly after death, and had changed positions at least twice within a very short period of time. So, the place of death was probably within half hour to an hour from the hospital. Time of death had been placed between 10:00 p.m. and 11:45.

I picked up the phone after Doc hung up, and I dismissed the team. I dialed Nathaniel's chambers. I expected to work well into the night, going through Joanne's house, and would not be able to keep our dinner date. Fortunately, I had fallen in love with a man whose professional duties had often forced him to cancel our social plans, so he understood when I canceled. I had often wondered if it was possible to have such a fulfilling relationship, based on mutual respect and nurturing. Since I didn't think such a relationship was possible, I hadn't gone looking for one. This one had taken me by surprise.

I had met Nathaniel when I testified in a criminal case in his court three years ago. I was completely fascinated by him before the case was sent to jury deliberations. I already knew of his impeccable reputation before that day, but had never met Nathaniel in person. Although I was aware that he was in his early 40's, I somehow expected him to look older, more staid or stodgy. He had wavy, mahogany hair that to grow to almost collar-length. His eyes, which appeared brown from a distance, were actually a golden hazel, with flecks of green and gold throughout the iris. Although I couldn't see the eyes up close during the trial, I detected a sparkle in them that spoke of intelligence and wit. While he conducted the trial with dignity and seriousness, Nathaniel did not hesitate to offer an encouraging smile to a frightened witness. He smiled warmly at the jurors as he gave them their charge, and congratulated them on their patriotism for serving their honorable duty. I found myself thinking how willing I would have been to serve jury duty in his court.
His black judge's robes camouflaged a well-toned, muscular physique, and accented his darkly handsome appearance. I had responded to his magnetism as any warm-blooded woman would to such an attractive man. But I was impressed more by his calm, firm, yet fair judicial manner in trial. His sharp mind displayed itself repeatedly throughout the proceeding. His stern persona surfaced when he chided attorneys for behavior he found unacceptable in his court. The eyes which sparkled with warmth could just as easily snap with anger, if provoked. I found both facets of his personality charming.

Unlike celebrity judges who primped and posed for television cameras, Nathaniel banned the cameras from his courtroom, and concentrated on making fair, well-reasoned rulings. Although I had been skeptical at first, he had proven to me over time that he was as balanced, fair and down-to-earth in his personal life as he was on the Bench.

Nathaniel sounded disappointed that we wouldn't see each other for our date, but told me he understood about my commitment to the Cavenaugh investigation. Before signing off with a husky, "I love you," he asked me to call him when I got home, so he would know I had arrived safely. I loved the way he balanced caring and nurturing without smothering me, or detracting from his respect for me as a professional officer of the law, capable of handling myself in an emergency. I felt cherished and protected without being patronized or paralyzed. God had been very good to me with this man.

Chapter Four

Forensics had made little progress on the bits of evidence by late afternoon, when I stopped by to check on the status. The team members promised to take turns staying late during the course of the investigation. Casts of partial footprints and a partial tire cast were available for my review. I was amazed that they had been able to salvage anything from the trampled, muddy crime. They had recovered more detail than I thought possible.

Three distinct types of shoe prints showed up in the casts. Two men's size tens, appeared to have been made with the same athletic type of shoe, with cushioned soles and high arch supports. Harry, the evening lab tech and I theorized that they could be from the orderly's shoes. I made a note to have Rosini and George check it out. Although the type and size of shoe were identical, one appeared to be older and more worn than the other. One of the prints looked a bit strange, almost like there was a smaller print in the middle of it. I theorized it was probably from commingling of prints at the scene, complicated further by the unstable, muddy ground. The third partial print was smaller, roughly a men's size eight. The sole was smooth, with no added arch support. I suspected it belonged to Rosini. So far it appeared that the partial prints would not be of much help to the investigation.

The tire print would be compared with the squad car and Rosini's car. Deep inside my Detective's intuition, I knew that it, too was tainted evidence, and would offer little or no clue to the murderer's identity. Damn Rosini and his sloppy scene processing! Everything negative about the investigation seemed to come back to him. I was beginning to sound like a broken record, even to myself.

A gray curtain of dusk descended as I drove to Joanne's home. I flipped on my headlights and the radio. The past twelve hours seemed like four, yet like an eternity at the same time. I was tired, but not sleepy. If only my body could keep up with my mind. A gnawing sensation in the pit of my stomach reminded me I had forgotten to eat all day. I was running on adrenaline and caffeine, not an ideal chemical formula for brain fuel. I turned into the nearest fast food joint and ordered the healthiest meal I could find on the menu. I balanced it in one hand, and ate while I drove. As I neared Joanne's address, the road dipped into a low area, and descended into fog. I put my broiled chicken sandwich on the seat next to me, and strained to see where I was driving. Dusk abruptly dropped into one of the darkest nights in my memory. Instinctively I reached up to pat my side, where my service revolver rested in its holster. The cold steel calmed my raw nerves.

Joanne's house sat off the road by roughly half an acre, in an unincorporated area north of the city limits. The yard was neatly clipped and edged. I wondered how she had managed to keep it so immaculate and still keep vigil at her mother's bedside. My tires crunched along the gravel in the circular driveway, as I inched closer to the house. Visibility was next to zero. Suddenly my headlights focused on a car ahead. There was Joanne's car, parked at her home, as though nothing had happened, and it waited for her return.

Suddenly I didn't want to be there by myself. I wasn't afraid, or was I? I didn't want to officially request a back-up, so I dialed the station and asked the deputy at the night desk to connect me with the forensics lab. If Joanne had made it home last night, then this could have been where she encountered her killer. I asked Harry to send a team to the house to collect evidence as soon as possible.

Had I not been so intent on proving to myself that I wasn't afraid, I might have stayed in my car with the doors locked until the forensic team arrived. Instead, I grabbed my flashlight and rubber gloves from beneath my seat, patted my gun , and quietly got out of the car. Balancing the flashlight under my arm, I pulled on a glove before trying the back door. It was locked. Remembering the key Father O'Brian had given me, I retraced my steps and returned to my car to fish for it in my purse. I sat half in, half out of the car, with one foot on the floorboard and one on the driveway, as I shone the light in my purse with one hand and rummaged with the other.

A choking feeling rose in the back of my throat as gravel crunched behind me. I jerked my foot into the car, and grabbed the door handle to pull it shut, but it wouldn't close. A deep chuckle, followed by the appearance of Rosini's face in my window made me loosen my grip on the door handle. At the same time, an involuntary sigh escaped my lips. I hadn't heard his car, and only heard his step when he was directly upon me. A mixture of anger and relief flooded over me, and my hands trembled slightly as my fingers finally closed around the key in my purse.

"Rosini! I think I'm very happy to see you!" I nearly shouted. My enthusiasm surprised both of us. "You didn't waste any time getting here. Is the forensic team on its way?" I asked. He gave me a puzzled look that said he didn't have any idea what I was talking about. He said he had decided to join me at the house on his own, and had not been back to the station since he and George left the hospital. He was also bearer of the sad news that Hannah Cavenaugh had died while he and George were at the hospital.

"Well, I see we wasted a lot of time searching the hospital garage, didn't we?" he pointed to Joanne's car. "How did it get here?" I assured him I had no more answers than he did at this point.

I cleared a place for him to sit on the passenger's seat, and motioned for him to join me while we waited for the forensics team to arrive. He declined my offer to share my half-eaten sandwich.

We had a lot of material to digest before we could make sense out of the case. For a short time I almost enjoyed Rosini's company, observing fleeting glimpses of what our deceased colleague saw in him as a friend. I hoped by the time we solved her murder, that Rosini and I would start a new, less adversarial chapter in our professional relationship.

Meanwhile, I wanted to glean anything Rosini knew that could help us find the killer. I knew he was close to the case, and might not see as clearly as he could, if he was a distant observer. So I asked, "Rosini, can you think of <u>any</u> motive anyone might have for this senseless killing?" Everything I've heard so far paints her as someone you would never expect anyone to harm."

"I don't have any answers, Sam," he sighed. I was surprised that he addressed me by my first name. He usually called me by my official title, or Ms. Larsen, lacing them both with a sarcasm.

There was no hint of sarcasm in his voice tonight, just sadness and weariness.

I couldn't help but feel a bit of compassion for him. "This is pretty rough on you, isn't it?" I felt a pang of conscience for resenting him so much, as I continued. "You know, we're on the same team, Rosini. We both want the killer caught. So, why don't we bury our differences, at least until whoever did this is brought to justice, and actually work <u>together</u> for a change. We don't have to like each other, just cooperate with each other. And when this is over, if you still want to antagonize me, I'll be happy to reciprocate." He grinned a little, and I felt better. When I extended my hand, he shook it.

He gave me a rundown on what he and George had found out at the hospital. It wasn't much, but maybe a hidden piece of the puzzle lurked somewhere in the information, and it would have more meaning later. The orderly, Jim Mason, had been called in on his night off, at approximately 3:30 a.m. to replace a coworker who had suddenly become ill. He had been asleep, alone, when the charge nurse called and woke him up. George had confirmed all of this when he talked to the nurse who made the call. The nurse aide who had become ill was at home, and would not be on shift again until the weekend. She had no phone, but George was going to pay her a visit in the morning.

Mason was a Respiratory Therapy student, who worked nights at the hospital to support himself while going to school. He lived in a basement apartment around the corner from the hospital. The upstairs residents owned the house, but were away, enjoying their retirement, as they were much of the time. Mason earned a 50% discount on his rent by keeping an eye on the house and doing yard work while they were gone. He claimed he was studying, alone, from 9:00 p.m. until he went to bed sometime shortly before he was called in to work. Although he had no alibi for the time of the murder, Rosini and George had found nothing to make them suspicious of him. They concluded that he had seen nothing unusual that could help lead to the killer.

Rosini had talked to the ER nurses and doctors, and George had tracked down all ambulance drivers and paramedics to see if anyone had seen anything suspicious in the area from 10:00 p.m. on. All of the people interviewed had said essentially the same thing…they were too absorbed with emergencies to notice anything outside the emergency room. A few of them noticed the routine Security patrol or police car making rounds from time-to-time. Nobody noted the time of the patrols, since they were used to seeing the patrol car making its rounds, and felt secure, rather than suspicious, by its presence. Rosini agreed to check the security company's logs and the City police logs to follow-up with the officers on duty that night.

The forensics van arrived just as Rosini concluded his report. I hoped our truce would hold throughout the remainder of our investigation. I didn't tell Rosini or anyone else that there was a possibility Joanne was a random victim of a serial killer, or that I had worked on a similar case in Texas. I wanted to pursue that part of the investigation by myself, at least until I could compare evidence from the Texas case with this one to see if they might be related. So far it seemed there was nobody who remotely harbored any animosity towards the victim, so there was an absence of motive.

After a thorough dusting of the doorknobs and windows for prints, forensics allowed us to enter the house. They stayed one step ahead of us with their evidence gathering and photographs. One of the team members noticed possible footprints outside the master bedroom when he was dusting the window for prints, so he poured casts. When I looked at the area, I agreed that there might have been prints at one time, but didn't see how he could harvest any distinct prints after the rain. After the impression material dried, he picked it up, pointing with agitation to a small area I had not noticed. There on the edge of one partial print was the perfect imprint of an entire thumb, and the partial image of two fingers, at mid-knuckle level. At first glance the shoe prints bore the same unusual irregularity as one of the large, athletic type shoes found at the hospital alley site.

Other partial prints matched muddy overshoes in the kitchen, probably worn by Joanne at some time during the storm. The thumb and finger imprints in the mud were small and delicate, almost the size of a child's. I suspected they would turn out to belong to Joanne. Forensics hooked up a bright spotlight to their portable generator and combed the area for minute scraps of evidence. I surmised that the prior evening's violent storm probably had washed away most evidence, but if anyone could find clues, they could. I was only mildly surprised at the end of the night to see that they had found scraps of clothing clinging stubbornly to a piece of bark, and a tiny, dark piece of cloth or leathery substance, which almost matched the surrounding mud, embedded in one of the footprint casts.

One cup and one saucer stood in the dish drainer on the kitchen sink. Both were clean and dry. Forensics bagged them, along with a clean saucepan, resting upside down beside them, to take to the lab for further examination. Since none of the bloodwork was back from Joanne's autopsy, nobody knew if she had been drugged or poisoned, as well as being strangled. They would check for traces of chemicals and prints.

While forensics combed for evidence, Rosini and I went from room-to-room in the house to see if anything was amiss. The decor spoke volumes about the house's occupants, more than anything I'd gleaned from documents and interviews to date. It was apparent that the two women possessed a sense of domesticity. The sweet, subtle scent of cinnamon wafted from small, exquisitely decorated baskets of potpourri which had been discretely placed in each room. Handmade doilies graced polished oak tables, and the top of an upright antique piano. The rooms were dominated by large, cozy furniture. Except for a light film of dust which had settled over the sheen of highly polished wood, everything in the house appeared untouched and immaculate.

Rosini volunteered that he had been in the house a few times as a guest. He said he noticed nothing missing or out of place, but also added that he didn't pay attention to details when he had visited. I would have to check with Father O'Brian to see if he would go through the house with me to determine if anything was missing. But, if it was, it was not immediately evident. The bed was neatly made, and clean towels hung neatly in the bathrooms. Nothing seemed out of place. There was no sign of forced entry.

I had felt from the first time I saw Joanne's brutalized body, that this murder had been very personal. For one to strangle a person they must be up close and personal, and judging from the force her killer had applied, there was a lot of anger towards her. It spoke of overkill. Now, finding the murder scene, set in a remote area, I was more convinced than ever that this was personal, and had been committed by someone she knew. As an introvert, her sphere of friends was small. She socialized when necessary, but shared her loyalty and prized friendship with very few. Nearly everyone who knew her, liked her. Few people set out to randomly kill a stranger in a remote site. There was the Kansas killer in "In Cold Blood," but there was an associated motive for those murders. Joanne had been killed during a blinding thunderstorm. Perhaps a stranger had been stranded in the storm, and knocked on her door for help. I saw no evidence of tire tracks other than Joanne's but asked the forensic crew to check tributary roads for signs of a disabled car or other tracks, just to be sure.

A tow truck arrived to take Joanne's car to the lab for a thorough examination, and we left shortly afterward.

Chapter Five

Father O'Brian did a marvelous job with funeral arrangements for Joanne and Hannah. Each detail bore the loving, personal touch one would expect to be absent for two women who had no surviving next-of-kin to mourn them. Matching white caskets sat side-by-side, their closed lids draped with sprays of delicate pink rose buds and fragrant white gardenias. A color portrait of mother and daughter, taken many years earlier, rested in an ornate frame, perched on a small table next to a flower arrangement. Rays from afternoon sunlight filtered through the stained glass windows in the sanctuary of the quaint, Catholic church, casting a soft, pink glow. Subtle, white light reflected from hundreds of candles strategically placed throughout the sanctuary.

I was equally surprised at the number of mourners in attendance. I had expected only a handful of friends from the

Sheriff's department, but every pew in the church was filled. I recognized a few people, but many were strangers to me. License plates on many of the cars in the parking lot were from out-of-town..

Rosini sat in the first row, along with the other pall bearers. His back was to me, but I noticed his head bowed forward several times during the service, even though his back remained poker straight. I asked Father O'Brian, who sat next to me, about the other young men in the front row. A couple of them appeared to be no older than teenagers. Only one wore a suit and tie. The others were clean and neatly groomed, but wore more casual attire. Some were in clean, but faded blue jeans, with tennis shoes and casual shirts. They all sat reverently still, and carried out their pall bearer duties with utmost dignity and seriousness. The priest explained that these young men were part of an inner city literacy program which the church sponsored. Both Joanne and Hannah had volunteered as tutors for the disadvantaged youth who benefited from program.

Father O'Brian kept his head bowed and eyes closed during most of the service, which Father Hanson conducted. A small choir of young boys sang several hymns. Catholic members of the attending crowd partook of the Holy Communion, while non-Catholics silently watched. The processional following the hearses to the cemetery was considerably smaller than the crowd which had packed into the church for the funeral. But the crowd gathering at graveside filled the canvas-covered area, and spilled out onto the gravel driveway. Father O'Brian conducted a brief service there, ending with a simple prayer of benediction.

"Detective Larsen, please wait," I looked towards the voice to see a conservatively dressed, slender brunette walking quickly towards me as I left the graveside service. Her face was partially obscured by the veil attached to her black hat. Her high heels, clopping in the gravel like a graceful Shetland pony, increased their tempo as she struggled to catch up with me. I glanced behind her at the crowd still gathered at the graveside, and noticed Rosini staring at her with an angry scowl on his face.

As the mystery woman moved closer in my range of vision I thought she looked remotely familiar, but couldn't recall where I had seen her before. She introduced herself as Julie Anderson, a name which meant nothing to me. Noting my blank expression, she quickly identified herself as Rosini's ex-wife. I didn't recognize her after all, since she had moved away from the area before I arrived. She had remarried since leaving Iowa, and wore a large, square-cut diamond solitaire, with simple gold band on her left hand. Her mannerisms, speech pattern, classic dress and carriage presented someone from an old moneyed background, with years of training at the finest preparatory schools. What a contrast to Rosini's clearly blue collar, middle class upbringing.

"Please pardon my intrusion on your private grief," she panted, still trying to match my stride. It was the proper sentiment, spoken with perfect diction and grace. She continued, "I need to talk to you about the Cavenaugh women...and Robert. And please, don't tell Robert about this." Now she had my curiosity thoroughly aroused. I agreed to meet her for coffee at a small cafe a few blocks from the cemetery. It hadn't occurred to me that she might know the deceased. But it made sense that she did. I knew from the look on Rosini's face as he watched her walk to her car, that he was aware of our contact, and quite angry about it. But if he asked about it, I could give a perfectly rational reason for talking to her. She was merely a background witness I had decided to interview while she was in town. Besides, except for my promise to Ms. Anderson, I didn't care what Rosini thought. His opinion meant little, if nothing to me.

Mrs. Anderson was already seated at a small corner table when I arrived at the cafe. As I approached the table to join her, I glanced out the window near her in time to see Rosini drive by. I wondered, Did he still carry a torch for her...or was it something far more sinister? Why would her presence, and my meeting with her agitate him so much?

"Detective Larsen, thank you for meeting me." She seemed in a hurry to unburden herself, and began to talk almost immediately as I sat down. "I feel I must warn you about Robert... Well, not so much warn you, but I think you need to be careful with Robert."

I admitted that Robert and I were not fans of one another.

"No", she continued, impatiently, "I don't think you understand. Robert doesn't dislike you, personally. He hates what you stand for, an independent, in-charge woman. His mother was just the opposite. I never met her, but Robert's father told me all about her. He and Robert adored her. Robert is basically like his father, except Mr. Rosini did not develop a cruel streak after Mrs. Rosini's death. Robert did. Robert also canonized his mother after her death. He turned what was a loving, warm relationship into almost... a worship of her, I guess. In his mind, she transcends a human role, and is almost equal to the Holy Virgin Mother. I cannot explain fully what I am trying to tell you."

"How does this affect me, other than explaining why I grate on Rosini's nerves?" I asked. "He doesn't hide how he feels about me or other professional women. I know how much he resents me for being promoted, instead of him."

"Do you really? I mean, you may know he resents you, resents your promotion, but do you <u>really</u> know Robert? He is a man with very deep hurts, deep resentments, and he holds a grudge forever." She lowered her eyes as she spoke, and then closed them tightly. I asked her to explain.

"Robert wanted to play sick, uhm... games, when we were married. Sometimes he begged me to punish him, and he sometimes called me 'Mother' and I don't think he always knew it was me." The unexpected switch from warning me, to discussing her sexual life as Rosini's wife took me by surprise, and obviously made Mrs. Anderson uncomfortable. She blushed, avoided my eyes, and fidgeted with her napkin. Her clear, articulate speech became halting and awkward, with numerous pauses. She must have believed it was important to tell me, though, because she continued.

"Other times, Robert tried to... punish me. He used his handcuffs to cuff me to the bed, and he, he used a leather whip on me. And he talked vulgar to me, too, almost looked like a different person, like he was demon possessed, if you can believe in such things. I don't mean literally. It's just the best way I can describe how he became. He is a very sick man."

She continued, describing bouts of violence, triggered by simple acts or omissions, like the time she forgot to pick up his dry cleaning, or when friends unexpectedly dropped by, and Rosini thought the house wasn't clean enough for company. He managed to inflict pain, without leaving physical evidence, like bruises or cuts on her body. Mostly, the abuse was psychological. She described a hellish nightmare that no woman could endure for long and keep her self-esteem intact. She had been treated for depression, and had even contemplated suicide while married to Rosini. Reliving the stress and abuse caused her face to lose its serene beauty as she talked. Small lines appeared around her mouth and eyes, and she appeared to age ten years in a few minutes.

I decided I'd heard enough about Rosini's character. It made me uneasy, yet confirmed inner intuitive suspicions I had harbored about him for some time. It was time to talk about the deceased. She had, indeed known Joanne and Hannah Cavenaugh.

Joanne and Rosini were hired by the Sheriff's Department at the same time, and met during new employee orientation. Apparently Rosini had charmed the shy Joanne, because she seemed a bit less shy around him than she did around most other people. She was only six or seven years older than Rosini, but she seemed much older, and Mrs. Anderson thought Joanne somehow reminded Rosini of his mother. He doted on her, and she reciprocated. There was never any suspicion of an affair. Rosini separated women into two categories: either the sainted Madonna-mother figure, or the whore. Joanne and her mother both filled the sainted role for him. Julie mused that she undoubtedly filled the role of whore, as would any wife or lover.

She confided that she was afraid Rosini might become obsessed with finding Joanne's murderer, and that he might mentally snap during the process. She feared for me. I represented too many negative symbols to his twisted mind. Although she hadn't taken psychology in college, I thought she had accurately analyzed Rosini. So, I listened intently as she warned me to be careful. Working with Rosini was even more of a mine field than I had originally suspected. He could explode at any number of emotional triggers, harming whoever detonated one of them. I agreed with his ex-wife that I represented too many potential triggers to take lightly.

Sometime between my second and fifth cup of coffee I asked Mrs. Anderson about how Rosini's mother had died. I had been curious for many years, and the subject seemed to fit in with whatever we were discussing at the time. Rosini never sought counseling for his grief, and had repressed and denied it instead. Yet, there was no way he could have avoided suffering terrible emotional damage from her death.

According to what Rosini's father had told Julie, on the day of her death, Annabelle Rosini had gone fishing with Rosini and his father. Although she had never learned to swim, she occasionally went out on the lake in the family's fishing boat, to be with her men. Deathly afraid of water, she was always careful to wear a life jacket, and was very careful not to sit too close to the edge of the boat.

Rosini was fifteen at the time. He was not a large man and was even smaller as an adolescent. But he was in good physical shape, and an excellent swimmer. His father also sported a compact physique, but was quite muscular, until cancer robbed him of his health and vitality many years later.

The day of fishing had been successful and fun. Annabelle hated the water, but loved her husband and son, and so had enjoyed herself immensely. All three were in a jovial mood as the men guided the boat into shore. Nobody understood why Annabelle took off her life jacket a few feet from shore. They guessed that she probably thought they were closer to the dock than they were. She was standing upright, laughing, when the boat bumped the pier, jolting the occupants, and throwing her off balance. She fell into six feet deep water, a mere three feet from shore. Both Rosini and his father dove in after her, attempting in vain to save her.

Annabelle's extreme fear of the water caused her to panic, and instead of allowing them to pull her to shore, she fought them with superhuman strength. Neither man thought to knock her unconscious. They both revered her so totally, that hitting her never crossed their minds, even in an emergency. Young Robert Rosini had spent the day clothed only in swim trunks, and was bare from the waist up. His mother had clawed at him in her panic, covering him with hundreds of deep scratches on his torso, arms and face. She had kicked and grabbed at his father's face, nearly drowning him, as she pulled him underwater, while he attempted to pull her to the surface. To their horror both Rosini men watched Annabelle drown that day, unable to save her. When their minds had cleared, sometime after the body was recovered and buried, both men blamed himself and the other for her death. They drew away from each other, and never fully reconciled.

I thanked Julie Anderson for taking time to tell me about Rosini. I didn't think any of the information would help me find

Joanne Cavenaugh's killer, but it helped me understand the man who was so determined to be involved in the investigation. I had suspected Rosini was cruel, but only in a vague, non-specific way. The cafe meeting confirmed my suspicions and gave form and substance to what I had not been able to put my finger on before.

I knew I couldn't use any of the information Julie had given me in a tangible effort to remove Rosini from the investigation team. The Chief would simply remind me that it was hearsay, and the source was an ex-spouse, who might have an ulterior motive for telling me what Julie had told me. I didn't think she had any sort of ulterior motive. In fact, I sensed she was afraid of Rosini, and what he might do if he found out about our conversation. If I read her right, Julie Anderson was genuinely concerned for my welfare, and had risked her own well-being to warn me. For her sake, I hoped she and her new husband would leave town immediately and not come back.

Chapter Six

The funeral and my afternoon chat with Julie Anderson left me feeling like a wrung out dishrag. Five cups of coffee had failed to infuse me with energy. As the afternoon light faded to twilight I fought with myself, wanting to go back to the office and work awhile longer on the Cavenaugh case, yet too exhausted to move. Somehow my car found its way home, and allowed me to park it in our driveway. I stumbled inside, flopped down on the couch without turning on a light or listening to voice mails. I convinced myself I would take a short nap, eat dinner and go back to work. Instead, I ended up falling asleep, and not waking until morning.

Even though I had slept deeply, it wasn't a restful sleep. Images of Joanne Cavenaugh, her bluish face and swollen, protruding tongue, paraded through my dreams. Another bluish face, a similar swollen tongue, which had spoken with a Texas accent, danced in and out of those dreams, sometimes replacing Joanne's, other times lying down beside it.

I was still tired when I awoke. Somehow one of my shoes had fallen off my foot as I thrashed about on the couch. The spiked heel gouged my back, prodding me to sit up. My navy blue suit was drenched in sweat, the skirt twisted around my waist and wrinkled. Having never mastered the art of getting panty hose all the way up without twisting one of the legs, or running a fingernail through the waistband, I chose to wear the old fashioned stockings with garters. Nathaniel thought this habit was sexy. This morning, however, I felt hobbled by it. Somehow my garter belt had come unfastened, and one stocking sagged at my ankle, while the other was twisted at my knee. My blouse was not in much better shape. It was unbuttoned, and I had apparently torn a button off during my tumultuous nap. Every muscle in my body felt like I had wrestled a burly opponent all night long.

The room was chilled, with a drafty wind playing through the living area. Rays from the morning sun spilled in through the partially opened front door. I must have been more tired than I remember, since I could have sworn I had closed and locked it when I came home.

I felt groggy and confused, a little afraid. Although I'd had nothing but coffee to drink, I felt hungover. Could I have been attacked while I slept? Or had I merely been careless, allowing my exhaustion to play tricks with my mind, convincing it that I had locked the door, when I hadn't? It didn't make sense. If I had been attacked, what was the purpose? The house was intact, and I could detect nothing missing or out-of-place. In spite of a growing uneasy feeling, knowing that something was amiss, I dismissed my suspicions, and convinced myself that my imagination was merely working overtime. I filed the uneasy feeling away in my mind's attic, where it could not interfere with the urgent task of putting together the pieces of the Joanne Cavenaugh murder puzzle.

The perpetrators on a few of my homicide cases had engaged in a mental cat-and-mouse game with me, pursuing some sort of pathological need to win a battle of wits, or prove a misguided sense of mental superiority. This game, if there was one, so far didn't quite match the earmarks for that type of game. In the past, they always left an obvious clue, to let me know they were challenging me. That could be what had happened here. But there was no note or taunting phone call. Knowing that the scene where Joanne's body had been dumped was staged, I knew we obviously had a murderer with a message, but the target of the message was still unclear.

I chose to ignore that he or she also had a message for me, and dismissed the condition of my clothes and house as mere oversight.

I pulled my skirt down, stood up, and hobbled to the bathroom. But not before tripping over my purse. It was lying open on the floor, across the room, halfway between the couch and the doorway to my bedroom. Its contents were strewn neatly on the floor next to it, making it easy for me to take inventory. Nothing was missing, and nothing was added to it. I found only one item in the vicinity of my living room which was out-of-place. While scooping up the contents of my purse, I snagged a small, thin, blue rubber fragment which appeared to have come from a shattered balloon. I knew the fragment did not belong in my home. I didn't recall ever having a balloon in my home for any reason.

For a moment I thought about calling forensics to take prints, but decided against it. I picked up my belongings from the floor and neatly tucked them back inside the purse instead. I discarded the rubber fragment, and emptied the trash.

As I stripped off my wrinkled clothes I glanced at my home phone, which t indicated I had one voice message. But the light wasn't blinking. That was odd. When I had left the house yesterday morning I had no messages, so I knew this was a new one. I had not listened to any messages the night before. The light always flashed when there was a new message, until someone picked it up and listened to it. If someone had listened to my message, why had they not erased it? I wouldn't have known the difference. I pushed the play button and listened. "Hey, Sam, I know you won't be turned on by the sound of my voice, but this is important." The caller was right about that. I hadn't spoken to Dan, my ex-husband for two years. We had agreed to stay out of each other's lives. Had we not become romantically involved, we probably could have remained friends, and I would probably still be in Texas on the police force there. But we were like moths to a flame. We couldn't stay away from each other, yet we couldn't keep from destroying each other. I didn't hate Dan, and he didn't hate me. We were just too passionate for a long term relationship.

Dan's message was disturbing. "Sam, this is strictly police business." I had to admit, Dan was an excellent cop. He would put personal feelings aside if police business required it. "It's about your strangulation case up there. I heard about it on the news last night. Sounds a lot like the Griffin case that you worked on down here. Thought you should know, and this is really weird, someone from the City police force up there requested copies of the Griffin file three weeks ago. Call me. You know the number. It hasn't changed."

I could check one item off my "to do" list for the day. I had intended to call and request the Griffin file as soon as I got to my office. Someone had elevated that item to top priority on my list. I wasted no time in dialing Dan's number. He gave me the name of the city officer who had requested the file, along with the fax number where he had sent it. He had already faxed a copy of everything in the file to my personal home computer. I pulled up the file and started reviewing it while he and I talked.

"Sounds to me like you have a rogue cop." He echoed my own thoughts. Why would someone ask for the file on an unsolved murder in another state, three weeks before a similar crime was committed in our area? I could think of only one possibility. I drew on Dan's years of experience as a homicide detective, asking his opinion on several issues in the Cavenaugh case. I hadn't had time to organize my thoughts and formulate a plan or hypothesis until our conversation. He helped me sort it out, and clear my mind.

I was so comfortable discussing the case with him that I decided to confide in him about the condition of my clothing and house when I woke up this morning. Big mistake. He swore under his breath. "Sam, don't be a fool. You've got to get forensics over there. None of that was an accident or coincidence, and you know it. I know you. You never would have left your door unlocked. You have to start following your hunches. They're valid. Don't let anyone make you doubt yourself. You are a darn good detective. You know I respect you, no matter what has happened between us." The Dan I had once loved, always respected as a cop, my mentor in the science and art homicide investigations, spoke out loud what I had not wanted to suspect.

I didn't tell Dan that I had already destroyed any evidence that might have existed. What else could I do? I didn't want to put my sanity in question during this investigation. One unstable detective on the case was enough. What did he expect of me? Should I go to the emergency room and ask them to run semen tests to see if I had been raped? I could hear it now. "No, I'm not sure if I have been or not, I just woke up to find my clothes messed up, my door open, and my purse across the room, dumped on the floor...No, I haven't been drinking. My occupation? Homicide detective."

I deliberately wiped the phone, the door, my purse, and all of the living room furniture clean of any prints that might have been on any surfaces, just in case I had a change-of-mind and decided to report it.

During my time on the Texas police force I had been assigned to several rape cases. The victims almost always said they had felt dirty and violated, and wanted to shower. I had kept them from washing away physical evidence until after their medical exams, and had not fully understood the urgent need for cleansing…until now. I soaped down three times, running the hot shower over my body until I depleted the reserves in the hot water heater. The cool spray on my face yanked me back to the present, and kept me focused as I dried off and dressed. I seldom dressed in heels and hose, and my body rebelled when I did. So this morning it was jeans and tennis shoes, and the most comfortable shirt I could find

I needed caffeine, but couldn't bear the thought of drinking coffee. After an extended session with the toothbrush and mint mouthwash to rid my mouth of the prior evening's stale coffee aftertaste, I brewed a strong pot of tea and poured it over ice. To this unconventional breakfast drink I added a banana and peanut butter sandwich on cracked wheat toast, my favorite comfort food. .

Feeling a bit confused and somewhat vulnerable, I decided I needed to talk to Nathaniel before heading off to work. As I lifted the phone from the cradle a new blinking red light caught my attention. I must have had a call while in the shower. To my surprise, it was from Julie Anderson. I thought she would be on her way to Michigan by now. Her voice sounded strained and upset. She talked rapidly, and was out of breath. "Detective Larsen, I just want to warn you, I think you are in danger. Someone didn't like it that you and I talked yesterday. A squad car ran my husband and me off the road last night as we were leaving town. I didn't see the driver. He shone his spotlight in our mirrors so we couldn't see him. But, I don't think it was Robert. It didn't look like a County car. Take care of yourself. Bye."

I replayed the message several times, my body numb, the world around me moving in slow motion. When I finally snapped out of my state of suspended animation and dialed Nathaniel's number, there was no answer. I pushed the speed dial button for his office number. It rolled to the court administrator's number. She informed me that he had an early pre-trial conference, and would not be available until the afternoon.

Instinctively I dialed long distance to Texas. Dan answered on the first ring. This time I held nothing back. Information and emotions poured out of me, as I barely paused to breathe. I no longer knew who I could trust here in Iowa. But I knew, for all of our differences, I could always trust Dan, the cop. He and I could never again be sweethearts, but we had always been a dynamic detective team. Even his presence via long distance telephone link was comforting.

When I had finished unburdening myself, Dan calmly instructed me to go to another phone to call him back. He didn't want me calling him from my home or office to discuss sensitive matters. I hadn't thought of the possibility that my phones or house might be bugged, but it was a reasonable suspicion. It might explain the condition of my clothes and purse when I awoke – a brilliant distraction. I wasn't convince that my cell phone was secure, either, so I drove to my church, and was allowed to use the youth minister's land line to call Texas.

When I finished talking with Dan I felt calmer, more assured, yet more cautious. We had brainstormed every possible angle we could imagine for the case, based on evidence and circumstantial occurrences to date. I was ready to tackle the investigation with a clear mind and steady resolve now, instead of being scattered haphazardly about by the various pieces of information which had landed in the case like small explosives, fragmenting my attention into many directions. Dan and I had pieced together an algorithm of evidence, similar to the algorithms used by paramedics and ER team members when they respond to heart attack emergencies. By following a flow chart format, we could play " If this - then-this," cover the various scenarios, remain focused and organized, yet still have room to deal with the unexpected. I was finally ready to go to the office, immensely grateful to Dan, as he offered his assistance any time I needed it in the future.

I placed two more calls before leaving the church. One was to Gene Rollins an ex-cop, private investigator who specialized in detecting and purging wire taps and bugs. I agreed to meet him at my house after work for a sweep of my space.

Then I reluctantly dialed the Chief's number. I wasn't prepared for his response. Chief was usually calm, personable, and professional. Today he was curt, impatient and rude. "Where the hell have you been?" he nearly shouted. "I've been trying to reach you all morning. Something very interesting has come up, and you'd better have a real good answer for it." I was as surprised that it was almost 11:00 a.m. as I was by Chief's outburst. I had spoken to nobody at the station, and had been on the phone with Dan for nearly an hour. It was uncharacteristic for me to be out-of- pocket without letting someone know my whereabouts. But my unavailability, alone could not explain Chief's agitation. I wondered what he was referring to, and for what I'd need a real good answer.

"I'll explain everything when I see you in person," I told him, still unaware of what had stirred his ire. I know that surprised him, too. I wasn't acting like myself. But circumstances dictated this change. I might as well go all the way and totally upset him. "Chief, I need to meet you alone, away from the office, and you must not let anyone know about our meeting. I have a very good reason, I promise." I set up the meeting at the church chapel.

As agreed, Chief arrived within the hour. He wasted no time in slamming a set of documents in front of me, and demanding an explanation. I barely stifled a surprised reaction. Then I took a matching set, which Dan had faxed to me, out of my briefcase. Chief and I started to talk at the same time. "Where did you get these?" I finally got a chance to talk. Someone had anonymously put them on Chief's desk. He wondered why I had kept secret something as important as the Griffin case. "Chief, I hadn't originally planned on keeping it a secret," I explained. "I wanted to compare the case file with the Cavenaugh information before sharing it. But now, I think it should be kept secret, with only you and me working on this aspect of the case." In response to his puzzled look, I explained about the request for the file three weeks prior to the Cavenaugh murder. His jaw fell open when I told him the request had come from within the city police department. He didn't recognize the name of the person who had requested it. That seemed odd, since Chief knew everyone at the City and County departments. I had already called the police switchboard and asked for the mystery person. The operator said nobody by that name existed on her directory. The fax machine which had received the requested file was a bona fide number.. But it was a mystery who had picked it up when it arrived.

Chief shared Dan's assessment that we had a rogue cop on our hands, even before I told him about Julie Anderson's message about being run off the road by a city police car. Something Rosini had told me about his part of the investigation at the hospital clicked in my mind as the Chief and I talked. The only vehicles anyone had noticed near where Joanne's body was dumped were either police cars or security vehicles. Rosini was supposed to follow-up and get logs from both entities to see which units were in the area from 10:00 p.m. until the time Joanne's body was discovered. I intended to follow-up with him on that assignment, without sharing information about the Griffin case or Julie's complaint with him.

Before we left the church, Chief and I made arrangements for regular meetings outside the office, and away from our personal phones, in order to follow the leads which we couldn't share with the rest of the investigative team. Rosini would probably think we were having an affair, I mused to myself. For once, Rosini's skewed thinking could be used to my benefit.

Chapter Seven

It was difficult meeting with the investigative team in the afternoon after my meeting with the Chief. It was difficult withholding information from them, but it was necessary. Until we identified our rogue cop, and determined his or her involvement in the Cavenaugh murder, we were forced to suspect everyone. There were enough assignments to keep everyone busy on relevant pieces of the investigation, so the piece the Chief and I kept hidden didn't impede the work.

Forensics had cast prints from orderly, Mason's shoes. Rosini agreed to have his regular shoes cast as well, so the prints could be compared to prints from the hospital alley. He seemed extraordinarily cooperative. I was grateful.

I asked Rosini to check with Father Hanson about the literacy program the church sponsored, to see if anyone tutored by Hannah or Joanne hadn't turned out as well as those kids who were pall bearers. He surprised me by complimenting me for the idea.

I planned on taking Father O'Brian through the Cavenaugh house to see if anything was missing. The remaining team members were assigned check out any police cars or security officers who were in the vicinity of the ER the night of the murder. Rosini had obtained logs from the Security company, and handed those over to Paul. He agreed to give the police logs to George to follow-up, so he could investigate the literacy program participants.

I watched Rosini out of the corner of my eye as I asked Pete to follow-up with everyone who had signed the visitation book for the Cavenaugh funerals. His lack of reaction, in light of his knowledge that I had met with his ex-wife struck me as strange. His venomous looks at her and his drive-by snooping at the cafe told a different story. What could have brought about this change? Was he pre-occupied with his current assignment, or had he decided to let go of his malice towards her for the duration of the investigation? Perhaps hearing me assign another officer the task of interviewing people who had attended the funeral, put my meeting with Julie Anderson in perspective for him. I was just too exhausted to care why he had changed. I cared only that he had changed, even temporarily.

I expected my visit with Father O'Brian to bring a routine, uncomplicated ending to a day that had been anything but routine. I could not have been more wrong. When the front door opened in response to my knock, I had to look twice to be sure I had the right address. The old priest who greeted me at the door of his living quarters looked terrible. Grief had taken a tremendous toll on him. The gracious, energetic, vital man who had just days earlier arranged a lovely farewell memorial for his friends, and had presided confidently over their graveside service, had been replaced by a feeble, frail, very aged man with ashen skin and disheveled white hair that begged for a comb. Matching patches of white stubble sprouted on his hollow cheeks and chin. Dull, blue-gray eyes sat above deep, dark, swollen circles. They seemed to peer out of sunken caves, with only a flicker of light touching the inner parameters. He looked more like a skid row drunk, in the midst of a drinking binge than a respectable spiritual leader. His eyes brightened slightly when he recognized me. When I told him why I had come, he agreed to accompany me to the Cavenaugh house. But the flicker of pain which flashed across his eyes told me that too many memories lingered at that house for him. I worried that he might not be physically up to a visit. Had I not needed the information he might be able to provide, I would not have pushed so hard.

"Please come in for a minute, while I freshen up a bit," he invited with a quivering, anemic voice. I followed him through the darkened hallway to a sitting area. He flicked on a small lamp, and offered me a chair. Instead of going to another area to tend to his grooming, he sat down in a chair next to mine. "I must talk to you before we go, Detective. I believe I have information you need." He paused, silently made the sign of the cross, bowed his head, then faced me, and continued in a faltering, weak voice, choked with emotion. " You see, I think I am responsible for Joanne's death." Surprise slammed into me, nearly knocking me breathless.

"What do you mean, Father? Are you telling me you killed Joanne?" I was incredulous.

"No! Lord, No!" his last statement carried more energy than I thought possible. "I would never knowingly harm her. I just should have told them no..." His voice suddenly strangled to silence. A bony, wrinkled hand grasped his chest. The ashen color intensified around his lips, while the tiny amount of remaining color drained from his cheeks.

He gasped for breath and attempted to continue, his eyes conveying an urgency to communicate which transcended his physical pain. Perspiration dotted his upper lip and forehead. It wasn't difficult to match his symptoms with those I'd learned in cardiac life support class. He slumped forward, and I caught his frail body in time to ease it onto the floor. Grabbing my CPR mask from my purse, I phoned the paramedics. Less than a minute had elapsed from the first onset of heart attack symptoms and the beginning of my resuscitative efforts.

The priest's living quarters, like the Cavenaugh homestead, sat several miles outside of the city limits. The Township fire department was several minutes away. I knew his chances of survival decreased dramatically each passing minute without defibrillation to shock his failing heart. I knew CPR alone wasn't going to save him. In a calculated, yet desperate move, I slammed my fist into his breastbone, delivering the precordial thump which could either stop his heart completely, or restore adequate rhythm to pump blood again. It was a gamble I didn't like to take, and would not have taken if there had been a defibrillator closer than six minutes away.

My gamble paid off. The old priest suddenly drew a breath on his own, and I detected a faint, yet regular pulse. I kept his head tilted back to keep his airway open, and kept a close watch to make sure he continued to breathe. After what seemed like an eternity, I heard the wailing sirens approaching. "Father, don't you die on me!" I ordered. "I need your help, so you hang in there." I moved aside as paramedics rushed in, a choreographed routine of efficiency. I watched in slow motion as they quickly assessed his vital signs. One team member attached an oxygen mask to his face, another methodically slapped heart monitor wires to his chest, while a third member started an IV. "ST elevations, with obvious Q waves," the team leader said as he pointed to the heart monitor. Not at all surprised, I knew those tracings confirmed his heart attack.

It didn't make sense to be angry with the old priest, but I was. He had been on the verge of breaking this case, and now he couldn't even talk. If he lived, it would be several days before I'd be allowed to talk to him. What else could go wrong with this investigation? I didn't want to know. I called the Chief from Father O'Brian's house. After explaining what had happened, I asked him to run a check on the priest through his FBI sources. We had better find out on our own why he thought he was responsible for Joanne's death. Did he have a criminal record? Or was he referring to the church's literacy program? Maybe we were already on the right track, having Rosini check out the program's participants. The case file in my briefcase still begged for attention, too. How could the murder of a shy, nearly reclusive middle-aged woman, with no known enemies give rise to so many rabbit trails? I asked myself an even more puzzling question, which had no answer. If the Cavenaugh and Griffin murders were related, what did the two women have in common? Sarah Griffin had been a vivacious, socially active nurse. Far from reclusive or shy. the two lifestyles were as different as the two states where the murders occurred.

My phone rang as the ambulance sped away. I guessed from the phone number that Doc had finished his autopsy report, or that he had some of the labs back, and could give me a more complete picture of Joanne's murder. I was eager to get my hands on it so I could start my comparison to the Griffin case. I could hear him whistling in the background when his assistant answered my call. Doc was a talented classical pianist, who whistled while he worked. His nickname was derived more from that habit, and his similarity in temperament to Snow White's dwarf by the same name, than his professional standing. Some mornings, especially if his circadian rhythms were off, I called him Grumpy instead. This afternoon, he was in good enough humor to be Doc.

As I suspected, he had a written report for me. His assistant agreed to leave a copy on my desk, since Doc couldn't wait for me in person. He had been called to sub for the regular A & P instructor at the university, and was leaving early to brush up on the professor's lesson plan.

Doc enjoyed lecturing, and took delight in the students comparing him to a brilliant but absent minded professor. His sense of humor went beyond dry to downright dehydrated. Students didn't laugh at his jokes, they usually groaned, once they understood the punch line. The entire experience invigorated him, and offered temporary release from the darker, macabre aspects of his chosen profession.

I was relieved that he wasn't going to be there to give me the report in person. Usually I enjoyed bantering with him about a case. But this one was a bit different. I wanted to read the report for the first time without any commentary, and without interruptions. It was important for me to take in the whole picture unassisted.

I didn't plan on reviewing the Griffin case file until after reading Doc's report. I didn't think I needed to. Even though it had been several years since I had worked the case, it was one that a detective never forgets. I was fairly sure that I could still recall each piece in vivid detail. I had originally expected the comparison to be straightforward and uncomplicated. But that was before I found out that someone had requested the file weeks before the Cavenaugh murder had been committed. Now I had to try and decipher whether I was dealing with a serial killer who had resurfaced, or whether Joanne's murder was a copycat killing. One thing I already knew - both cases had in common, neither case had a discernible motive.

Chapter Eight

Blinking lights. I was sick of those today, too. The "message waiting" light on my office phone informed me that I had one, probably several, voice mail messages. My first message was from Nathaniel. "Sam, sweetheart, you are elusive prey today." Of course! I had nearly forgotten the retirement dinner for Judge Bob Donald tonight. I had a mere 90 minutes to transform myself from bedraggled and exhausted detective to a socially acceptable companion to one of our State's most respected judges. Well, my compulsive alter ego would have to be repressed by the spontaneous, yet dutiful dominant Samantha Larsen, who planned to be coifed, composed and charming in a little over one hour.

When I called Nathaniel's house he answered on first ring, sounding a bit anxious when he heard my voice, like he half expected to be attending the dinner by himself. He agreed to pick me up in an hour. I left the remaining messages untouched, dashed to my car and pushed the speedometer to the outer limits of legal, arriving at my house in record time.

Once again I congratulated myself on my wise decision to adopt a short hairstyle. A little shampoo, a little styling mouse, a touch of curling brush, and I had chic glamour beyond my expectations. Thanks to a quick encounter with a brief, steaming soak in the bathtub, I didn't look as droopy as I had felt when I left Father O'Brian's house.

My erratic eating schedule had trimmed a few pounds from my hips and waist, so it was a pleasant surprise to find my favorite black dress showed off the improvements. So impressed was I with my svelteness, I decided bold was better, and switched to a clingy red number, with a surprise slit from knee to mid-thigh. When I crossed my legs just so, I could flash an ever-so-subtle view of my stockinged leg, which generally elicited a positive reaction from Nathaniel. While our relationship lacked the intensity of my short but passionate relationship with Dan, it was comfortable to be with Nathaniel, and I felt we had something that could last.

I knew first-hand how a passion that flamed to incinerator level could burn out if one did not focus a sufficient amount of energy on dispassionate details which sustained a relationship. Dan and I had never lacked passion. But we had not confined our fire to a safe zone. It permeated our entire co-existence, consuming us in the process. We loved passionately, we fought passionately. We did everything passionately, nearly destroying each other in the process. I planned on keeping just enough passion in my relationship with Nathaniel to keep it interesting and fulfilling. But I carefully limited the amount of passion I would allow. We enjoyed restful, peaceful interludes together, without fire and tumult. A little flicker of flame tonight wouldn't be too bad. I was too physically and mentally depleted for much more. The red dress would have to do its part.

I heard the click of Nathaniel's key, then remembered that I had not only exterminated all electronic bugs, but had also changed the locks to my house. I ran to the door in stocking feet to let him in. I hadn't told him about my previous confusing encounter with the mystery visitor. I had no plans to do so, either. I had the PI on retainer to check the house weekly for bugs. I hoped I would only have to change the locks one time.

Nathaniel's eyes spoke fluent puzzlement. "Just precautionary," I assured him. "I decided if I couldn't be sure that the previous owners didn't still have a key, that I would install new locks. I have a key for you. Trade?" The key exchange seemed to erase a worry wrinkle which had creased his handsome forehead. He enveloped me in a tender, tight hug and held me close to his chest for a long time. Without shoes, I stood a good six inches shorter than him, so with arms around my waist, he half lifted me to bring me up to a level where chest touched chest, and our hearts beat on the same level. Then he tested to see if my "stay put" lipstick really lived up to its advertisements. It didn't. "Darling, that shade of red clashes with your power tie," I informed him, while attacking the lipstick smears around his lips with a Kleenex.

"We could forget about the dinner and stay here, if you like." he offered, with a hint of mischief on his face. He pulled me close against his body and kissed me again. "Mmm, I've missed you." he mumbled, trying to talk and kiss at the same time.

"Didn't your mamma ever tell you not to talk with your mouth full?" I teased. "No, we can't stay home. First of all, as the song says, I don't get dressed up for nuthun'. Secondly, it isn't politically correct for a future State Senator to skip an important landmark in an esteemed colleague's life, for 'personal' reasons."

I poked him lightly in the ribs, forcing him to drop his arms and release his grip.. Feeling years younger than I had just an hour earlier, I playfully skipped away to finish dressing and to call the hospital.

"Father O'Brian is in critical condition," the matter-of-fact pronouncement of the ICU nurse brought me back to earth. My fountain of youth potion had worn off too quickly. I suddenly felt tired again. "Is he able to talk?" I asked, feeling too cold and too impersonal for my own liking. "Detective Larsen," she continued, "He keeps calling for you, but the doctor said I am not supposed to let you upset him. So, call me tomorrow. Maybe he will be well enough to talk to you by then." I agreed to her terms, and she agreed to call me if the priest's condition changed.

After I hung up with Father O'Brian's nurse, I fought temptation to take Nathaniel up on his offer to stay home. I knew his plans would not be restful, though, and discarded the idea. I touched up my lipstick while poking my feet into heels that were a sharp contrast to my stodgy work shoes..

Samantha Kaye Larsen, the sultry temptress, whose hands never touched dishwater or a service weapon, emerged ready to charm the good judge's cohorts. This woman was several years older than the one who had skipped into the bedroom minutes earlier.

Nathaniel regaled me with stories about his week in court as we drove to the dinner. It was comfortable being with him. He never pressured me to give more than I was able to give to him or the relationship. I didn't feel like discussing the Cavenaugh case, so we didn't. I had lived that case twenty-four hours a day, even in my sleep for what felt like an eternity. I was ready for an evening's vacation.

Party mingling isn't one of my favorite sports, but nobody could have guessed it by my conduct. As the future wife of a future politician, I was determined to master the art of looking like I was a natural at the activity. I believed in Nathaniel. I knew our State needed someone like him to be involved in guiding its future. I gladly sacrificed my reclusive tendencies for such a worthy cause.

A handful of well-placed law enforcement officers scattered among the guests. Their approving looks told me they were surprised that I cleaned up so nicely. Compared to my usual uniform of pants or jeans and a simple shirt, the crimson number I floated into the party wearing, was a Pygmalion delight. Rob Jackson, an influential administrator with internal affairs raised one eyebrow, Star Trek style, when he eyed the leg-revealing slit. I pretended I hadn't noticed. I was sure he was planning to comment on the subject when he sidled up to me. I couldn't have been more wrong. He wanted to talk shop, and planned to share some light gossip with me.. I was grateful that the dim lighting hid the sudden blanching of my complexion. His tidbit of gossip meant nothing to him. But it registered with me like a jolt of electricity on a dry winter day.

Rob found it amusing that several small canisters of nitrous oxide, or laughing gas, had disappeared from the property room. You can buy the canisters, called Whippets, to use for whipping cream, but they had become one of several new crazes among the teen crowd, bent on getting high. They attached balloons to canisters and sniffed the gas from the balloons. The missing canisters had been confiscated when officers had raided a teen party a few weeks earlier.

Nitrous oxide creates a state of temporary, partial asphyxiation, so it has the potential for being quite dangerous, if misused. I had a low tolerance for it, myself. My dentist had to administer it very cautiously when he used it to relax me for dental procedures. If he gave me too much, too soon (usually what the average person considers a normal amount), I experienced a claustrophobic response, and suffered from severe headaches afterwards. It didn't take much nitrous or alcohol to put me under the table. With 20/20 hindsight I realized the hungover feeling I experienced the morning after the Cavenaugh funeral was exactly the way I felt after receiving nitrous at the dental office. Now I knew how I could have slept through the rearranging of my clothes and purse, and planting the bug in my house! All roads in this mystery seemed to point to one or more law enforcement connections, from victim to perpetrator, to conspirator. I was suffering from a bad case of justifiable paranoia. A sudden, sick headache assaulted me. I decided it was time for me to curtail my mingling and find my man.

The small amount of festive spirit which I had mustered for the occasion had just evaporated. I would paste a phony smile on my lips and endure the dinner. But, I wanted to go home as soon as possible afterwards. I had a file to review and compare with an old, haunting unsolved murder file from Texas.

Halfway through the dinner speeches I congratulated myself on how well I was holding up, and what a marvelous job I was doing at acting the relaxed, attentive dinner guest. My theatrical performance didn't fool Nathaniel even slightly. He reached under the table a couple of times to squeeze my knee in appreciation and reassurance. He didn't know what was bothering me, but he knew something had happened since we arrived at the party. I didn't even feel his hand on my knee the first time he squeezed. I spent the rest of the evening as a gussied-up marionette in a clingy red dress, an artificial smile painted on my wooden face.

My distracted mood was so obvious to Nathaniel that I didn't need to concoct an excuse to leave early. As soon as the last good-natured roast had been delivered, and the laughter died away, dessert was served, and we bid our good-byes, adding our congratulations to Judge Donald on our way out the door. Nathaniel's hand firmly supported my elbow as he guided me through the crowd to the parking garage. He slipped a protective arm around my waist and kissed my neck as we waited for the valet to retrieve his car.

Once we were in the car all facades dropped. He pulled me close, holding me more like a cherished sister than a sultry vixen that I had tried to be all night. I relaxed only slightly, but it gave him the encouragement he needed to open up a dialogue. "O.K., do you want to tell me about it?" He wasn't impressed when I feigned ignorance. But he let the subject drop for the time being. With a gentle kiss that started out almost platonically and ended up with some of the fire I thought I'd lost during the evening, we silently agreed not to talk until later.

Nathaniel pulled his car out of the garage onto a newly wet roadway. It had started to rain gently while we were inside. In contrast to the night when Joanne Cavenaugh was murdered, tonight's rain fell like whispers from heaven. The large drops sang a soft, mesmerizing lullaby, accompanied by the rhythmic swish, swish, of the windshield wipers. My eyelids fought with the leaden weights which pressed down from above, forcing them to close. I slumped against Nathaniel's comfortably broad shoulder and drifted into a twilight state more relaxing than any I'd experienced since the murder.

I was only slightly aware of being half-carried into my house by a pair of strong, gentle arms. Nathaniel deposited me onto my bed, then bent to remove my shoes. I roused slightly, but not enough to transition completely into consciousness. When he unsnapped my garter belt and started to remove my stockings, though, I transformed into a mad woman, kicking, scratching, and screaming for him to stop. I was fully awake in seconds. He grabbed me by the shoulders and shook me, shouting, "Sam, Sam, it's me, Nathaniel! What is wrong with you?!" I started sobbing against his broad chest the minute I entered reality. "Oh, no, I'm so sorry!" I touched a red welt I had inflicted across his cheek.

Once I choked out the last sob, blew my nose, and washed my face, it was time to face Nathaniel and own up to my own behavior. Both clearly told me I wasn't handling what had happened to me here in my own house well at all. I had thrown the episode over my shoulder, attempting to walk away from it.

But it had sunk a hook into me, and I ended up dragging it along like a weighty anchor.

Nathaniel sat next to me on the bed as I started to talk. "Do you want me to help you get into your nightgown?" He asked sheepishly. "That's all I was going to do. Honestly, I'm not some weirdo who would ever take advantage of you while you were asleep or unwilling." He gave me a small, worried smile that begged me to communicate. "Besides, it is just too much fun when you are awake." I finally half smiled, and then started crying again like a blubbering baby. I had never seen Nathaniel so worried.

I finally told him everything, in between sobbing fits and squirts of nasal spray to unclog my nose from so much crying. I had never seen Nathaniel flinch before. As I told him about waking up with a hangover, when I'd had nothing to drink, and finding my clothes half removed, my purse across the room, and my door open, a dark cloud descended on his face.

He grabbed me with a previously undisclosed passion, nearly crushing me in an attempt to hold me close to him, the entire length of his body pressed against mine. He tipped back on the bed, without releasing his grip on me, and held me close. Neither of us spoke. I thought I heard him quietly curse under his breath, but I didn't ask for clarification. He curled his body protectively around me, and gently rocked me, like an infant, caressing my hair, my shoulders, my back. I detected slight spasms of his chest, which told me he was silently struggling with powerful emotions. When he was finally able to speak, he assured me that he would never touch me in any way that would make me feel uncomfortable. We would work through the trauma together. He encouraged me to seek counseling, but I wasn't ready for it. I had a murder to solve. Stubborn Samantha was back!

I was convinced that my attack and the murder were somehow inexorably connected. When I found the murderer, I would find my attacker. I also felt a bit foolish for the way I had handled the situation, erasing all evidence that could have led to the attacker.

In my post-attack shock, I had destroyed evidence which might have led to a murderer. Nathaniel minimized that fact, but both of us gasped as we realized I, too could have been found with purple face and swollen tongue, strangled silently by a deranged killer. The cold, hard truth was that the killer wanted me to live, at least for now. If he hadn't, I would not be alive. Apparently he wasn't finished playing games with me, and like a cat with a wounded mouse, took perverse pleasure in batting around his stunned prey. Well, I wasn't through with him, either.

Nathaniel, kicked off his shoes, and stretched out on the bed next to me. He held my hand and reassured me, "I'll be right here all night. So you go to sleep now. I won't let anything happen to you." I was quick to obey. For the first time since the Cavenaugh murder, I completely relaxed and immediately fell into a dreamless sleep.

Nathaniel was still there, watching over me when I awoke. I smelled coffee and cinnamon in the distance. He had cooked breakfast, showered, and shaved. But I didn't doubt that he had kept an eye on me the whole time. He looked like he hadn't slept all night. My heart swelled with love for that man. I told him so, too, as I pulled off the wrinkled red dress, and stepped into a steaming shower. After the soapy rivulets of water had washed away my grimy, salty feeling, I stepped out onto a fresh towel, and noticed my fleece robe had been discretely draped over the towel rack. True to his word, Nathaniel was giving me plenty of space to work through my feelings and find my way back to my comfort zone. His wisdom and patience were their own form of passion, and they aroused mine.

I heard a quick tap on my door. Then it swung open and in walked Nathaniel with a breakfast tray, loaded with juice, coffee, cinnamon toast, and scrambled eggs. He had also picked one of the pansies from my flower bed, and placed it next to my silverware. I felt almost human when I finished eating.

He waited for me to finish before changing from light banter to a more serious subject of conversation. "Uh, Sam....I thought of another possibility for your attack and maybe even for the Cavenaugh murder." It wasn't like my golden tongued prince to stumble over his words. He was clearly uncomfortable with what he was about to tell me.

"Now I realize this might sound really egotistical, but before you think I'm a clod, please think about it. I didn't want to think it was possible, but.... O.K. I guess there's only one way to say it. Maybe someone is trying to get to me. If they are, it is certainly working." He stopped to take a breath while I digested what he had just said. It was true. Nathaniel had made no secret about his political aspirations, and his fairness on the Bench must have made enemies of someone. The only people who had no enemies were those people who stood for nothing, who lost their integrity by trying to please everyone. Nathaniel didn't buy into that philosophy, even though he was a political hopeful. He always said he lived by the standard of, "Do what's right and honest and just, and that will stand by itself." In the three years we had been dating I had never once seen him waiver from that standard.

"O.K." he continued "Everyone around here knows you and I are an item, and you are going to be my wife. So, maybe they are trying to get to me by hurting you. Either the murder was committed to distract you and make you look bad, by linking the unsolved Griffin murder with this one...two cases you have worked on, or they are really planning to hurt you, and are just playing games right now, using the murder as a way to get to you. What hurts you, hurts me. If they discredit you somehow, they might discredit me. Or maybe they are trying to make me act in your defense - which isn't going to be hard to do- and discredit me that way."

He made sense. It might explain why someone requested the Griffin file before the Cavenaugh murder took place. The Griffin case was high profile in both Iowa and Texas. Sarah Griffin was a native of Iowa, and had been murdered near the campus of the Texas nursing school where she was a student.

My face had been plastered all over the Iowa newspapers for months. The final article conveyed the sad news that no suspect had been found. We had followed thousands of leads. I had worked round the clock with a top notch investigations team for weeks on end. But I viewed it as a failure, and so did many people in both states. I always hoped it would still be solved, and the murderer brought to justice. The bitter gall of frustration welled up in my throat, as it had for years every time I thought of the unsolved case. I was determined not to have two unsolved murders on my head. If they were in any way linked, I intended to solve both.

After Nathaniel left I called the Chief, using our pre-arranged code for a professional meeting out of the office. I had been so upset, I'd forgotten to tell Nathaniel about this aspect of the investigation. I hadn't told Chief about my mysterious attack, either. I still debated whether I should or not. If my phones were tapped again, our conversation would sound like a date for a romantic rendezvous. I'd better tell Nathaniel the next time I saw him. My private words and actions had a way of surfacing publicly when I least expected. I also told Chief I planned to work at home all day, reviewing the Griffin files uninterrupted.

Chapter Nine

I fully intended to work at home except for my meeting with the Chief. But as the old proverb goes, "the best laid plans of mice and men..." I had just finished setting up an Excel spreadsheet on my computer, to compare the evidence in both the Griffin and Cavenaugh cases, when my phone rang. It was County Hospital's cardiac intensive care unit. Father O'Brian was awake and had asked to see me. The nurse who delivered the message warned me that he was very weak, and his condition was still serious, but he seemed more agitated by not being able talk to me than if he was allowed to see me. I told her I was on my way.

Before I could get out the door my phone rang again. This time it was the Chief. I had intended to call him while I drove to the hospital, but he saved me the effort. I changed our rendezvous point and the time.

Chief delivered a surprise. His FBI source had just reported findings of his background search on the priest. It seems that O'Brian's life had literally begun fifty-three years ago, when he had moved to Iowa. That left twenty two years and another identity unaccounted for. A piece of bonus information left me similarly dumbfounded. Hannah and Joanne Cavenaugh had similar missing years. Joanne was only missing four years of her life, but Hannah Cavenaugh had begun her existence in our county fifty one years ago. That left a few decades unaccounted for. No further records were available to track down the missing years. However, the pattern fit what I'd seen before when people had taken new identities under a witness protection program. But their pattern predated the federal program. I suspected, whatever program they had followed had kept Hannah and the priest alive for half a century. Whoever had sent them into hiding had done a darn good job, sophisticated or not. I hoped the old priest would bare his soul and tell me what I needed to know. If the Cavenaughs and the priest had been in some sort of program, I found it odd that it would come back to haunt them now. But anything was possible.

My drive to the hospital took longer than expected. First my car refused to start, then I noticed one of my tires was low, so I decided to detour to a nearby Station in the opposite direction from the hospital, to pump it up with air. Halfway there, the tire completely deflated, so I had to change it. Had my car trunk not been loaded down with miscellaneous junk, necessitating completely unloading it to get to my spare, I could have changed the tire in less than ten minutes. It took thirty instead.

By the time I got to the hospital, Father O'Brian was unconscious again. I paged Chief and changed our rendezvous point to the CCU waiting room, so I could be there if the priest woke up. It was probably the most private place available to us, anyway. Fortunately for the citizens of our County, business was slow. The CCU had only one other patient and it appeared from the deserted condition of the waiting room that she had no anxious relatives, eager for the ten minute visiting privileges every two hours. I had saved my Excel document to my flash drive, so while I waited for Chief or the priest, or both, I popped it into my laptop, spread out the Griffin file on a nearby desk, and proceeded with my data input. I had forgotten very little over the years. I could almost input the information from memory. But I wanted to comb the data with a fresh eye to make sure I overlooked nothing, no matter how small or seemingly insignificant.

Chief arrived just as I was putting the Griffin case papers in a neat stack in my briefcase. I showed him the spread sheet and explained what I was doing and why. Chief is not computer literate, and half-way through my explanation I noticed his eyes had glazed over slightly. He claimed to have understood the principal, if not the details of the project. I could tell he was impressed, probably more than he should have been. Excel was a simple program. My project was a simple project. I simply abstracted the evidence in each case, entered it on a spreadsheet, then sorted the data so the program prepared a comparison. I had used this technique before, and usually was pleasantly surprised at how methodically it all came together with the click of a little button. I hoped when I finished with the Cavenaugh-Griffin comparison, I would be equally as pleased as I had been in the past.

My meeting with Chief was otherwise uneventful. He was discreetly investigating within the city police force to determine who had requested the Griffin file, and why. He had been with County for over twenty years, and had developed a few trusted contacts in that time span. By nature and experience he was a cautious, suspicious man, who trusted very few human beings, regardless of occupation. So, if he trusted a contact, the person must be beyond reproach. So far his investigation had yielded nothing at all. I could tell he was puzzled and frustrated. Those two adjectives summarized my feelings about the entire case. I recalled seeing a bumper sticker that expressed my feelings, and smiled as I silently adopted it as my motto. "God give me patience, right now!"

Chief's phone rang as we were concluding our uneventful meeting. Unlike me, he seemed to enjoy being interrupted. Chief had a few years and a lot of patience over me, in his favor. He noted the number, with a smile on his face, told me. "This may be the break we've been waiting for," I tried to piece together what was being said from his end of the conversation, but "Yep, uh huh, well, I'll be….Yeah, be right there." just didn't do it for me.

Chief flashed me one of his lopsided, tobacco-stained grins as he ended his conversation. His contact at City had a solid lead on who within the Department might have requested the Griffin file from Texas. I invited myself to accompany him to the interrogation of the suspect. Like it or not, he accepted my invitation. I often suspected that I amused the old man, even though I knew he respected me. I knew I took myself entirely too seriously, and he knew no matter how many times he pointed it out to me, I wouldn't change. So, we entered into a tacit agreement of mutual respect, and let each other's annoying nuances alone. Too bad marriage couldn't be like that, I silently mused.

Chief and I walked together to our cars, speaking little on the way. He knew very little of the details of his contact's investigation within the police department. As we were to discover later, locating and apprehending the suspect was almost unintentional and accidental. We had all operated from the assumption that the party requesting the file had been a police officer. Not until the amateur computer hacker attempted to brazenly access a highly secured data base, did anyone suspect that the culprit might be otherwise. As a temporary clerical hire, filling in for someone who was out on maternity leave, he was not listed with the switchboard directory, either. That explained why I came up empty-handed when I inquired.

Chief took an emergency detour to replenish his nicotine supply en route to the station, so I arrived shortly before he skidded into the parking lot. I sat for a few minutes and watched squad cars pull out of the driveway, wondering how the hacker would tie in to the mysterious City squad car which tried to run Julie Anderson off the road as she left town following the Cavenaugh funeral. Gaining access to a 2000 pound vehicle was a bit more visible and noticeable than plugging codes into a computer, or requesting information by telephone. We had so many promising leads, yet so little solid information in this case. Surely something would break soon.

An unlit, filterless cigarette hung loosely from Chief's lower lip as he peered in my window and tapped on the glass. He motioned for me to leave my briefcase and laptop in the car, so I locked both in the trunk. Grabbing my purse, I trotted along beside him, keeping double time to catch up with the effortless strides of his long legs. Chief stood nearly 6 feet 2, and I'd wager his legs took up about four feet 6 of that height. I don't imagine he came close to being handsome, even in his youth. Bronzed leather skin and gnarled, rough hands told the story of an Iowa farm boy who had worked the fields and tended the animals, probably when he was as young as grade school.

There was a difference between the Chief's wrinkles and those worn by Rosini. Chief's appearance and character spoke of decades of hard work, his skin roughened by cumulative decades of exposure to sun, wind and harsh Iowa winters. Rosini's premature aging originated from within, and spoke of bitterness, pain, and rebellion against the hand dealt to him by life. The crevices in Chief's facial map followed tributaries from smile lines around the mouth and crinkles around the eyes from squinting against the sun. Rosini's accented a pouty mouth and a chronic frown on the forehead. He personified the internal cannibalism of hatred.

I was breathing pretty hard and beginning to perspire by the time Chief turned in to one of the interrogation rooms on the second floor. I'd missed several mornings of my usual morning run, and took it as a warning that I'd soon be out-of-shape if I didn't get back into my routine. On a conscious level I'd told myself I was too busy to run. But I knew the real reason, even if I couldn't put it into words. My skin still crawled when I thought of that morning, and my imagination tried to fill in details I could not remember.

At first glance I thought Chief had mistakenly turned into the wrong room. This one surely housed a petty theft or misdemeanor flasher suspect. The pasty-faced, gangly young man, whose complexion was generously sprinkled with adolescent acne could not be a serial killer or even a copy-cat killer. The pale blue eyes hiding behind oversized horned rim glasses flashed intelligence, but also fear of a trapped, wild animal. An anemic attempt at growing a mustache sat in disarray on his thin upper lip. The same pale reddish color as the unkempt series of cowlicks sitting atop his skull, it barely registered as hair. I had to look closely to see if he had grown whiskers, or had drawn it in with an eyebrow pencil, or if it was a strange color of Kool-Aid, which he had failed to wipe from his mouth. Lanky, stork-like legs twitched beneath the table, accompanied by the percussion beat of long, bony fingers, drumming restlessly on the table. Fingernails bitten into the quick were rimmed by halos of raw, chewed cuticles. I doubted this much damage had been done in the short time since he had been apprehended and brought to the interrogation room. This young man was a wiry sinew of nervous energy. Chief and I exchanged looks that told me he shared my skepticism.

Chief's contact, a seasoned Internal Affairs investigator named Abel, led the interrogation. Danny Peales, the suspect, was twenty-two, about four years older than I had guessed. He worked through a temporary agency while attending college, where he majored in accounting. He had taken a couple of computer science classes, and spent most of his spare time surfing the net on his home computer. So far, nothing was a surprise.

Suddenly the dam broke. Peales lower lip quivered, waterworks of tears tumbled over the spill-way, and he began babbling, out-of-control. His respiratory rate nearly doubled, and I feared he would pass out from hyperventilation if he did not finish his story quickly. There wasn't much of a story to tell. When he finished, Chief, Abel and I unanimously agreed that he had told the truth.

Peales was Sarah Griffin's younger cousin. Having read too many "Three Investigators" and "Nancy Drew" stories in his not-too-distant youth, he had decided to investigate Sarah's death himself, and felt confident he could solve it using his computer knowledge. He had discussed the murder and his desire to investigate it on Facebook for several months, collecting advice from private investigators and amateur crime-buffs before landing a temporary clerical position at the police department. Bolstered by how easy it had been to have an out-of-state police file faxed to him at work, he had decided to go all the way and break into the secured police data base. The description of his bumbling investigative efforts matched his physical presence.

Peales' information raised as many questions as it answered. He knew nothing about the attempt to run Julie Anderson off the road. He didn't hide his thoughts or emotions well. A rather transparent, empty expression supported his stammered denial of any knowledge of the incident. When he read about Joanne Cavenaugh's death in the newspaper, he had recognized how similar it sounded to his cousin's murder. Fearful that he might become a suspect if anyone found the Griffin case file in his possession, he had shredded it in the office security shredder. Almost as an afterthought, he mentioned that he had misplaced the file for a short time. It had been missing for nearly two days, when it mysteriously showed up on his desk, with no explanation, and he had no idea who had placed it there.

Peales also knew nothing about the copy which had mysteriously appeared on Chief's desk. Chief had already sent the copy to forensics to examine for prints, and his were the only ones which appeared. They had, however, found minute traces of powder, intermixed with microscopic remnants of latex, confirming that whoever had placed the copy on Chief's desk had worn gloves, and did not want his or her identity known. So now we knew. The Cavenaugh killer, whether he was the same person who had killed Sarah Griffin or not, was a clever strategist, who was carefully baiting us with clues, then slamming the door in our faces as we approached the solution.

One more of his game pieces waited for me on my office desk. In a plain white envelope, void of fingerprints, but microscopic dustings of latex and powder, was one of the puzzle pieces from the Griffin case, which had been conspicuously absent in the Cavenaugh case - until now. Inside, as I expected, was a neatly printed message. The printing appeared to match what I recalled from the Griffin case. Instead of writing the message by hand, or cutting letters out of newsprint, as one often saw on TV, the Griffin killer had used a label maker, readily available at office supply stores across the country. I already knew the paper, as the envelope, would be void of prints, even before Forensics confirmed it. The taunting of years past had now entered this case. The killer, my tormentor, challenged me anew with a very familiar phrase, "And he ran and ran, saying, 'Catch me if you can, Bitch. I'm the Gingerbread Man'."

Chapter Ten

"Well, crap!!!" Chief sputtered. He didn't need to put his sentiments into words. I shared them already. "A Goofball computer Geek, who has put a case out on Facebook, then we get one just like it a few weeks later!" The thought overwhelmed me, too. "Now, how many thousands of times has he complicated this?" Try tens or hundreds of thousands. He admitted to having put the entire Griffin case file on Facebook, hoping to get information and guidance on how to solve it. The odds of it getting into the wrong hands were astronomical. Now we had to decide if our Cavenaugh case was a copycat or serial killer with thousands of potential complications.

Chief spat a soggy chunk of cigarette and mangled tobacco onto the grass. He continued with his tirade, language growing more colorful the more agitated he became. He was pretty predictable. By tomorrow he would have switched from cigarettes to cigars. We could always tell when Chief was on a big case or having to deal with a personnel issue that irritated him. He liked to chew vigorously when agitated, and his language took on a blue hue. He had tried chewing gum and tootsie rolls in the past, but he tended to swallow the gum and the tootsie rolls pulled off his dental crowns. So, he chewed cigars and cursed.

Chief had gone through a lot of cigars in the years since I had first met him. He and I had worked together on the Griffin case when I came to Iowa to check into Sarah's background during my investigation into her murder. My marriage to Dan was crumbling at the same time, so when the Texas police chief disbanded the Griffin case task force and it was placed among other cold cases, I had contacted Chief to see if he would put in a good word for me somewhere in the Midwest. He went a step further and hired me for his own department. Having participated fully in the Griffin investigation, he was aware that the investigation had been top notch, even if the case had not been solved.

I knew before I could begin to answer Chief's questions, I would have to review Joanne Cavenaugh's autopsy report in detail, and input it into my Excel program. It seems I had been interrupted each time I had opened the file. So I hadn't even once read it completely. I told Chief where I'd be and what I planned to do until this task was finished. He agreed to call me if he needed me, but otherwise he would feign ignorance of my whereabouts. I had to give priority to this task, or remain at a standstill.

Once home, I decided to take a quick jog around the block to clear my mind and my conscience, for neglecting my physical fitness for so many days in a row. The crisp autumn air invigorated me somewhat, and emptied some of the stress out of my psyche. Of course I thought about the Cavenaugh and Griffin cases as I ran. I couldn't help myself. Before I knew it one block had turned into two, and two into a mile. The sun was setting quickly, sending out its burnished tributaries as I puffed into the driveway, pleasantly soaked with perspiration, and filled with resolve to finish my Griffin-Cavenaugh comparison before I closed my eyes in sleep.

Before stripping down for a shower, I meticulously searched my house for unwelcome visitors, and double checked all of the locks. I had installed an extra deadbolt since my earlier nocturnal, unexpected encounter with the unknown and uninvited visitor. I put a pot of gourmet coffee on to brew, popped a Healthy Cuisine into the microwave, and ignoring my blinking message waiting light on my phone, stepped under the cleansing rivulets of my pulsating shower head. When I emerged twenty minutes later, I was ready to work all night, if necessary. And as it turned out, it was necessary.

Reading the Cavenaugh autopsy report, while eating with one hand, I was into my second cup of coffee, and had just swallowed my second forkful of rice pilaf with French green beans and almonds when I ran across an unexpected detail that would have caused me to choke if I had not already cleared my mouth. What the.......? I stopped and read it again.

Doc would have customarily brought something this bizarre to my attention, but he had been out of pocket when I had picked up my copy of the report. I didn't know what to make of it, even after reading it several times. So, I dialed his number, hoping he was still at work. His department had been unusually busy with a rash of recent auto accidents, so he hadn't gone home yet. He agreed to meet me at his office, sounding relieved to take a break. I rationalized that I was on official business, so I broke the speed limit getting there. I needed an answer.

"Coffee?" Doc held out a mug of what looked like last week's brew. I had enough caffeine and adrenaline cursing through my circulatory system at the moment, so I declined. We got right down to business. I had my copy of the report, and he had already pulled the file. He already knew, without being asked, which portion of the autopsy I wanted explained.

"You're wondering how a corpse, dead just a few hours, could have decomposed sperm in her vagina." Doc said matter-of-factly. Yes, that would be the question. Sarah Griffin had been either sexually assaulted or had consensual sexual intercourse, by a non-secretor, meaning the man who raped her didn't shed DNA clues into his semen. In the Griffin case, the semen had been fresh, and her sexual contact had taken place while she was still alive. Not so for Joanne Cavenaugh. Doc had already established that the vaginal abrasions inside the vagina had been inflicted post-mortem. Now, I find out that the semen had been old, with decomposed sperm! I'd encountered weird before, but I think this was a prize winner.

"Well, there are a couple of possible explanations," he continued. "First off, it is possible that her attacker was a woman. Therefore, unable to produce semen and unable to duplicate that portion of the Griffin case..." He hypothesized further that the abrasions in the vagina could have been caused by the introduction of something like a turkey baster or large syringe, which the killer could have used to deposit the semen. It wasn't too uncommon for some women who wanted to have a baby but not enough money to pay a doctor for medical insemination, to solicit donor semen from male friends or relatives, then to inseminate themselves, using an inanimate object like a turkey baster. If that was the case, someone out there besides the killer knew something about this case, and we might be able to entice them to come forward if we offered a reward for information. It was also possible that the killer was a male, who was impotent except when engaging in self-gratification. So, he had obtained his own semen, stored it, then introduced it into Joanne's body after killing her. As strange as the evidence, it didn't help us solve whether it was the calling card of a serial killer, or a badly duplicated piece of evidence by a copycat.

I was intrigued by Doc's final hypothesis. Perhaps the killer, either male or female, didn't want to use the semen of an acquaintance or of himself, so they had stolen semen from a donor center. He had certainly covered every possibility. I was grateful to have Doc's steel-trap mind on my side. I decided to check out the sperm banks in the area to see if there had been anything unusual, such as a break-in within a month of the murder. However the killer had obtained the semen, he or she had not been too careful with it, and had left it unrefrigerated for a significant amount of time. Whether that was on purpose or out of ignorance was unknown. Perhaps they had intended for the sperm to decompose so they couldn't be traced. We would only solve that mystery when we solved the murder itself.

Before leaving the morgue, I asked Doc to withhold copies of the report from anyone else, including police officers who might be working on this case. I had never asked him for a similar favor, and I knew it puzzled him. But he agreed, without asking any questions. Before I left he placed the Cavenaugh file in the safe in his office, so one of his staff would not inadvertently give out a copy without his knowledge. That isn't to say they hadn't already done so. I asked him not to find out at this point in time, but added that I might need to know if anyone else had a copy later in the investigation. I had a sneaking suspicion that one Mr. Peales had already obtained one, but I didn't want to have that on my mind at the moment. If I found out for sure that he had obtained one, I might have to join the Chief and start chewing cigars.

I knew once I finished my Excel spreadsheet comparing the two murder cases, I would have to figure out how to mitigate the damages he had spread via social media. I wasn't as familiar with technology as I had hoped to be. I surfed the Internet occasionally, when I needed specific information from governmental agencies, like the CDC in Atlanta, or the Department of Agriculture, or other agencies which freely shared non-classified information of general topics. But that was about the extent of it. I didn't come close to qualifying for Geek status.

Driving home I shifted mental gears and ran the information Doc and I had discussed over in my mind. I concluded that I needed to share it with the Chief first thing in the morning, but it would not become part of common knowledge shared with our entire task force. I hoped to convince him to let me put the case, minus such details as the vaginal contents, on the local TV crime-seekers show. If anyone out there knew about the semen, we wouldn't have to mention it. It was a long shot, even to get Chief to agree to it at all.

Generally when we did a Crime-Seeker spot we were inundated by calls and false leads for weeks to come. We didn't have the manpower assigned to the case to handle thousands of leads, in hopes of finding a valid one. County taxpayers were a conservative lot, and would not approve of us spending the extra money to staff up for a massive influx of leads, either. The County Sheriff's department was being held accountable for every penny it spent. In an era of corporate downsizing and cutbacks, the voters who paid our salaries would frown on extravagant spending to solve the murder of one person. It is likely that they would see it is wasteful and self-serving, since that one person had been a County employee. Unless we were willing to devote the same amount of manpower and money to every murder case we encountered, we were treading on thin ice to attempt it with the Cavenaugh case.

The evening newspaper had been delivered in my absence. I hadn't intended to read it, but I couldn't ignore the headline, *Local Murder Case is Deja Vu for County Detective.* I knew it was too much to hope that the local press wouldn't jump on the similarities between the unsolved Texas case, and the one at hand. Someone, probably Peales, had chatted with the reporter at length, and had done a pretty thorough comparison of the cases. I was correct about one thing. It was obvious that someone had already obtained a copy of Joanne's autopsy report. Every graphic detail was splashed across the front page. I wondered if Peales had put this information out on Facebook as well. Even if he hadn't, it would be history by tomorrow morning.

Chief's number appeared on my caller ID just as I unlocked my front door. My Crime-Seekers idea was instantly moot. We expected the leads to start pouring in before sun-up. The question foremost on my mind was how to screen them so we didn't end up with another Peales in our midst. He was already out the door, and in the ranks of the unemployed. But how many more would-be amateur detectives lurked behind seemingly innocent veneers? Worse yet, what if the killer found his way into our midst as a temporary employee, working on the very case he had created?.

I called the Chief. We agreed to meet at the hospital CCU waiting room in order to allay any suspicions we might raise with our rendezvous.

Chapter Eleven

Chief and I arrived at the hospital at shift change. The nurses were leaving as we entered the elevator en route to the CCU waiting room. A slightly familiar face smiled at me above the powder blue of hospital scrubs. "Detective Larsen! I'm so glad you made it. Father O'Brian was calling for you all day. I wasn't sure you got my message, since you didn't call or come by earlier." I realized one of the unanswered messages on voice mail must have been from this nurse. Before I could speak she continued," Of course you won't find him in CCU. He was transferred to a regular room earlier. As soon as he made it clear to his doctor that he didn't want anything heroic, and he went on DNR status, they decided he shouldn't be taking up CCU resources. Being DNR, we wouldn't be able to resuscitate even if something happened, so why have him on all those monitors, with all of the technology, right? So, Father Hanson gave him last rites, and he was moved to a private room away from the glaring lights, machines, and constant monitoring, needle sticks, and everything." She directed us to Father O'Brian's room, and Chief and I decided to visit the priest before finding another meeting place for our conference.

When we first stepped into his room, I thought Father O'Brian was either asleep, or that he had already passed on. His ashen, shriveled figure lay quietly in a bed that now seemed to swallow his frail body. I was amazed that a person could deteriorate so quickly. Someone had combed his wispy white hair, and it framed his still, wizened face like a cotton-candy halo. Without the shrill whine of monitoring machines or the whooshing, gasping respirator in CCU, I could barely tell if he was breathing or not. Then his eyelashes fluttered gently, like a butterfly caught in a sudden gust of wind, and tired, gray eyes fixed an intense gaze on mine. His bony hand motioned for me to come closer, so I did.

The bony hand grasped mine, with the strength of a newborn kitten. Pale lips curved into the hint of a smile, and a labored whisper escaped from them. "I'm so glad you came, Detective. I have much to tell you, and so little time. You must find who killed my Joanne. It is my dying wish." Like I wasn't under enough pressure to solve this murder. Now I had a priest's dying wish to live up to.

"I know you took many samples of hair, tissue and prints from Joanne's house, and sent them off for DNA testing. I will save you some trouble . You will find when you match some of the hair from the bathroom with Joanne's tissue that I am her father." I glanced out the corner of one eye to see if Chief had heard this information. He had quickened his pace chewing his cigar, so I guessed that he had.

"Actually, my dear, that is only the beginning of what I must tell you. But it ties in with why I think I caused my dear child's death. Joanne was conceived a few years before I ever became a priest. And I didn't even know about it until she was nearly four years old. You see, as a young teenager, I had pledged my intent to enter the priesthood, as I felt very strongly that it was my calling. But then, when I went away to college, I met Hannah. Her name was Hannah Livingston at the time. We were both from California, she from the Los Angeles area, and I from San Diego. We met at UCLA. I hadn't planned on falling in love. I had stayed away from girls during high school, planning to take a couple of years at the university, then entering seminary.

Hannah was lovely, but that wasn't what drew me to her. She was just different from the other girls. You see at that time, girls went to college to find a husband. Hannah went to college to get an education. She was so smart, so serious about life. Most of the guys in class were a bit irked that she got better grades than they did. But she didn't care. She wasn't one to pretend to be stupid in order to get dates. While most of her classmates pledged for sororities and fraternities, she chose to live in a frugal dorm room on campus, and worked evenings as a waitress to pay her own way. Her father was disabled, so her family couldn't afford to send her to school. Her tuition was paid by scholarship, and the rest of her expenses were paid by the sweat of her brow. She petitioned the dean to take nearly double the normal load of classes so she could finish school early. She didn't let up during the summer, either. She took advantage of all summer school could offer, and had close to two years of credits accumulated by the time we entered our sophomore year. She had taken bookkeeping and accounting classes right at the beginning because she planned to get a bookkeeping job by day and switch to night classes during her junior year.

So, you can see why I admired her. I came from a background of money, where most of what I had was given to me by my parents. But, they didn't overindulge me. I still had to work. They instilled a good work ethic in me from my youth. I mowed yards and did odd jobs around the neighborhood while I was growing up, in order to have spending money. My grandparents were poor Irish immigrants who had worked very hard to establish our family in America. Nothing came easy for them or my parents. We didn't take money lightly. I didn't have to work during college, but I was expected to get top grades. I didn't do too well my first semester, passing, but not excelling.

Hannah and I were part of a study group with five other students. We shared such background information with each other when we went for coffee after our study sessions. She took an interest in my academic status, and started coaching me to do better. I was impressed that she had the energy to care about how anyone else was doing, considering what a heavy load she was carrying. I never did tell her in the early days that I had plans to become a priest. I guess I was interested in her early on, and didn't admit it to myself. She seemed content to leave our relationship at a totally platonic level.

Hannah was too proud and determined to accept any financial help from me, even though I had plenty of spending money. So, on nights that she waited tables, I ate dinner at the restaurant where she worked, and requested her station. I'd leave a large tip for her, which she always tried to return to me when I came by to escort her home after work. One night when she was arguing with me about the tip I had left, I was just overcome by her and leaned across and kissed her to make her hush up. I hadn't kissed many girls in my lifetime, and I was completely unprepared for the intensity of my feelings for her. I didn't stop at one kiss, and she didn't try to stop me. Right there in front of the restaurant, we kissed and kissed. We lost track of time, and we didn't even notice people walking by and staring at us until a policeman came along and told us to move on. I drove her home and kissed her goodnight, but not before blurting out to her that I was in love with her. From that moment on I stopped thinking about becoming a priest, and started thinking about becoming a husband and family man once we graduated.

Well, our courtship started that night, and before long was too hot to handle. We were both very naïve about the birds and the bees. That just wasn't something you talked about in those days. We felt pretty confident that we could handle our relationship and stay out of trouble. But we were wrong. Each time we were together, we went a little further and a little further, until one night we went too far, and we both lost our virginity. We were both so ashamed. We promised each other we wouldn't do it again. But, of course we did. We were intoxicated by each other and addicted to our love. We decided the only decent thing to do was to get secretly married before the end of the semester, then later tell our parents and have a real, church wedding once we graduated.

I bought her a little ring, and we got our blood tests for our marriage license. On the day we were supposed to go down to the courthouse and get our license, my life took a drastic detour that changed things for both of us forever. I was taking her ring back to the jewelry store to get our initials engraved in it when I witnessed a murder. The jewelry store owner was robbed, then shot by two men. I saw their faces clearly, and heard them talking. They had real distinctive voices that I would recognize anywhere. They didn't see me, so I stayed hidden behind a pillar until they left. I then ran inside to try and help the jeweler, only to discover he was dead.

I called the police. When they got there, they took me out the back way to the police station, where I was able to identify the killers in a mug shot book. It seems that they were also on wanted posters in the Post Office. The police told me they were really bad characters, and that they were sure they were part of a very powerful crime family that had a lot of contacts around the country.

The last time anyone had witnessed a crime committed by that family or one of their hired help, the witness had been brutally killed, along with his entire family, his girlfriend, and even a member of her family. The police took me into protective custody and warned me against having any contact with my family or any girls I was seeing. I told them I was only seeing one girl, and that we had planned on getting married that week. They told me they would keep an eye on her without her knowing it, to try and keep her safe, but the best thing I could do for her was to never talk to her or see her again. Well, I loved her enough to give her up, if it meant she could go on living. So, I did what they suggested. I stayed in jail until I testified in trial against the killers. Then I moved out of state and created a new identity for myself.

I took all of this as a sign from God that He was unhappy with what I had done, and that I was supposed to be a priest, after all. So, I went into seminary with a totally different name. O'Brian is my false name. My real name is Peter Henry O'Conner. I finished seminary, was ordained, and the church moved me here. I thought everything was all set.

Then one day when I was on retreat in Oregon, I ran into Hannah. I nearly fell over in a dead faint! She had a young child with her, and I knew almost immediately that the child was my daughter. I didn't need to count on my fingers to realize that I had left Hannah behind, pregnant. At first she didn't recognize me. But it only took a second or two for the realization to hit her. There I was in my collar and black shirt. There she was with a child. I could tell she was getting ready to shout my name, so I quickly stepped as close to her as I could and introduced myself as Father O'Brian. Since she looked unwell to anyone who might have been watching, I took her arm and helped her to a park bench, while carrying her child - -my child in my other arm. I quietly told her while we were walking, that I would explain everything to her, but it would have to be clandestine, and she would need to refrain from calling me by my birth name. We met, as agreed, in a nearby church. Although she was not Catholic, and I was not a priest at that church, we sat in the Confessional and I told her the whole story. When I had finished, she told me she still loved me, and that she wanted to be with me. She told me what I already knew, that the child, Joanne, was my baby.

My heart nearly burst with love for the two of them. But I told her I had taken my vows as a priest before God, and I could not break them. Besides, I truly believed that God had permitted me to witness the mob crime to get me back on track to be a priest, and that He would severely punish us both if I quit the priesthood or broke my vows. Now that, Detective, is a very strong incentive to stay celibate! But I also had a responsibility to the child I had fathered. I was truly torn. I wanted so to watch her grow up, and to be able to see my Hannah from afar. So, when she insisted on moving to the Midwest, near my parish, I couldn't tell her no. I found out through my police friends that there were still members of the crime family who were not in jail, and their sources said there were many members of the organization who were still quite active in their lives of crime.

But, I am too human I guess. I didn't tell Hannah no. I helped her find a place to live and she found a job, using a false name. We sort of unofficially put her and the baby into a witness protection program of our own, without official help. I researched the County birth and death records until I found birth certificates we could use to get new identities. Then we got Hannah a new social security number. Joanne never knew any of this, and just assumed the identity we gave her.

I went to the owner of the construction firm where Hannah worked as a bookkeeper, and confided partially in him. Of course I fibbed a little, and didn't tell him the whole story. I couldn't risk it. I told him a sister parish had contacted me about a woman who had given birth to a baby before her husband was killed, and that someone very dangerous was trying to take her baby from her, so she'd have to take on an assumed name and move here. The owner, who was a faithful member of my parish, helped me relocate Hannah and Joanne, gave her a job, and protected her by letting her use a false name. To my knowledge he never told the secret of her identity to anyone, ever. I never gave him her real name.

I thought we were out of danger. It had been over fifty years since Hannah had assumed a new identity. Surely the entire crime family and their heirs had died or repented during that time. I became too bold, I guess, and started spending too much time with Hannah and Joanne after Hannah was diagnosed with cancer. I'm afraid I may have led the crime family to them. I don't know how. But, why else would someone have dumped Joanne's body right under my nose?"

He started to weep softly. My heart went out to the old priest. I didn't believe he had anything to do, even remotely, with Joanne's death, and I told him as much. He just smiled, as though he thought I was humoring a dying old man. I believed that Joanne's death was not connected to his activities as a witness against the mob.

It didn't make sense that someone who wanted to teach the old man a lesson would wait 50 years to do so. It didn't fit the pattern for retaliation. Usually retribution was meted out while the offense was still fresh on the offender's mind. If the mob had intended to deter others from turning State's evidence, why wait so long, when nobody knew about the incident that was being avenged? Why let him live a fairly happy life for so many years, then suddenly surface and kill his daughter? If our FBI contacts couldn't find out that Joanne was the priest's daughter, how could some remote relative of a long-ago crime family?

Joanne's body was dumped within sight of her father purely by coincidence. Sarah Griffin's body had been similarly dumped, behind the County hospital in Texas, eight years ago. In trying to recreate that crime, the killer had inadvertently convinced an old priest that there was a message in it for him.

I could see that the small amount of strength he had mustered for this conversation was fading quickly, so I asked one last question that I needed to know. "Father, I know you cannot go with me to Hannah's house to see if anything is missing." He nodded an answer, so I knew he was still listening even though his eyes were closed. "Did anyone besides you have a key to their house?"

He opened his eyes a slit, then struggled to answer. "When Hannah first went to the hospital, Joanne asked her police friend, the one with the Italian name-"

"Rosini?"

"Yes, that one. She had him look in on the place a few times. But she told me he snooped too much when he was there, and she didn't want him to go there alone anymore. So, she got the key back from him, and told him since I lived so close to the house anyway, and he had to drive so far to get there, that she had asked me to look in on things on my way home, instead. The key I gave you is the one she had originally given him."

"Father, how did Rosini act when Joanne took the key back?" I asked.

He didn't answer. All of his strength gone, the old priest closed his eyes and went back to sleep. I heard from the nurse later that night that he never woke up. The obituary stated that he had died quietly in his sleep sometime after midnight.

Chapter Twelve

Chief and I said little to each other as we walked to the hospital cafeteria. After the exhausting meeting with the priest, we didn't feel like going back to the CCU waiting room for our meeting. Besides, we both needed a cup of coffee. There was nothing like the bitter, dark brew we found there to clear our minds and wake us up. While we drank our doses of caffeine, I made a vague, unsuccessful attempt at levity. Smiling wanly, I looked at Chief and said, "Gee, we need to quit meeting like this." Chief's smile was even more tired than mine. Except I'm sure mine didn't have a piece of tobacco stuck between the two top central incisors.

Chief nodded at something across the room, and following his gaze, I noticed the orderly, Mason sitting by himself, slurping some of the watery chicken noodle soup which the cafeteria had labeled as soup de jour. He suggested that we postpone our meeting just awhile longer, and take advantage of the situation. We still had some questions for the young man.

Earlier in the afternoon, as I had been leaving my meeting with Doc, Harry, from Forensics had summoned me to the lab. He had been somewhat obsessed by the strange footprints we had found both at Joanne's house, and where her body had been found. He had studied the casts from all of the footprints and partials taken at both scenes. The normal prints had belonged to Mason and Rosini, but we couldn't figure out who the unusual, two dimensional print belonged to. It was the same size and type of shoe as the orderly's, but the depth was different, and it appeared that the tread on the sole was older and more worn.

Mason was deep in thought, engrossed in his Respiratory Therapy book when Chief and I approached. He jumped a couple of inches out of his chair when I spoke his name. " Sorry, Detective. I didn't hear you. Was trying to memorize this stuff on blood gases, you know respiratory acidosis, versus metabolic acidosis. Metabolic alkalosis versus respiratory alkalosis. Who would ever guess that the lungs and the kidneys work so closely to regulate body pH?" I nodded, not understanding a word he said. Now I knew how Chief felt when I talked about my computerized evidence projects.

I apologized for interrupting his studies, but explained to Mason that there were still some unresolved questions about the shoe prints, and we needed his help. Harry had suggested that we get prints of Mason barefooted, then send all of the casts to the lab for further analysis. He agreed, but said he had exams the next two days, and wouldn't be able to come in to the lab until he was finished.

When I asked him if he had any thoughts on how two such different prints could come from the same basic shoe, Mason looked puzzled. "I have no physical deformities that would cause part of my foot to hit differently." he said. "I think the bare footprints will show that. Look, I want to cooperate. It isn't fun having people look at me like I might be hiding something, you know. And about the other shoe. I think it could be mine. I had an old pair of shoes just like the ones I am wearing now, and was wearing the morning I found the body, kept them here in my locker to change into while I broke in my new ones. You know, to keep the blisters away. They disappeared from my locker about two weeks before I found Ms. Cavenaugh's body. I didn't think much of it at the time. I mean, who on earth would want my old shoes? I wouldn't want anybody else's old shoes. Afraid I'd get a fungus or something. I didn't report them or anything. That's just a little too weird for me, if you know what I mean. If somebody was so hard up to steal an old pair of shoes, they could have them with my blessing. I had just about broken in my new ones anyway, and had some old work shoes at home to wear for yard work and such like. But, I told that other detective this already. Didn't he tell you?" I looked at Chief. We both wore matching puzzled looks. Rosini had reported talking to this young man, but hadn't said anything about the missing shoes. True Rosini style, he had omitted details that he probably thought weren't important, but which could become pivotal to the investigation. We excused ourselves and left Mason to his studying. He agreed to let us know after he had his prints taken by forensics, and to call one of us if his missing shoes turned up.

Chief barely controlled himself once we were out of earshot from the orderly. "Just why did you put Rosini on this case, anyway?" he snapped.

"Me?!" I nearly shouted. "I didn't put him on the case! I didn't <u>want</u> him on the case! You know how I feel about his sloppy police work. And you know how he feels about me. Why on earth would you think I put him on the investigations team? I'd rather work *alone* than have him on my team! He was there at the scene before I got there. I just assumed you assigned him, since you were the one who called me." It became readily apparent that we had both been duped by one Robert Rosini.

"He was Joanne's friend, and probably knew we wouldn't let him on the team if he asked," Chief continued. I didn't care to be as understanding. He was right. I wouldn't have allowed Rosini on the team. He obviously wanted a piece of the action, and just chose to take it. Well, his game was up. I wanted him off the team!

"Well, I don't plan on letting him get away with it," I fumed. "I'm sick of his screw-ups and his snide innuendoes. I'm sick of his playing Rambo, and trying to show me up on this case."

"I'll handle Rosini," Chief said, jaw working the cigar furiously. "You know he will accuse you of picking on him personally, like he's done ever since you were promoted. I know, he's not exactly an enlightened man of our generation. He's still in the Ozzy and Harriet era when it comes to women's roles in society. I probably would be, too, if my wife and daughter hadn't boxed my ears all of these years, to bring me into compliance." Chief's wife was a nursing administrator at Mercy Hospital. His daughter was an assistant prosecutor at the District Attorney's office. Somehow I could visualize them dragging him, kicking and screaming into the age of women's rights and equality. He'd probably chewed up plenty of cigars in the process.

"Besides, Rosini sees me sort of as a pal, you know." He continued, spitting a chunk of soggy cigar into a napkin, and then wiping a trail of brown tobacco juice from the corner of his mouth. "We used to go fishing and hunting together. Still do sometimes. Haven't since you came, because I've heard his filthy insinuations that you slept with everyone who had anything to do with your promotion - including me." Chief would never have disclosed that piece of information if he hadn't been frustrated with Rosini. He even blushed a little bit after he said it.

"I still buy his custom-made hunting calls, so I think he still expects we'll go hunting together sometime." He quickly brought the conversation back to a neutral subject, away from anything personal. I wasn't aware that Rosini had any hobbies, but apparently he was quite good at imitating animal sounds with his little, hand carved wooden mouth harps. He was encouraged by the millionaire duck call family on T.V. and thought he had a shot at becoming rich from his own versatile animal calls. I let Chief rattle on about some of the water fowl he and Rosini had bagged, using Rosini's bird calls. When I perceived that he was no longer uncomfortable because of his inadvertent slip of the tongue, I pulled him back to the subject at hand.

Just what were we going to do about Rosini? He had inserted himself into the case obviously because he felt more capable of solving it than me. He was a detriment to this investigation, even though he had done quite a bit of the mundane footwork involved in following-up on leads we had received after the news story hit the papers, comparing the Griffin case to the Cavenaugh murder. He enjoyed doing so, since the article had cast me in a negative light. As our leads grew colder and fewer in number, Rosini had taken on some of the simpler investigation assignments for a couple of uncomplicated crimes of passion that had been committed since Joanne's murder. So, he didn't have daily contact with the case. I guessed the Chief would leave him on the case, but we'd watch him closer, and he'd caution Rosini to report everything, no matter how trivial he thought it was.

Rosini had reported finding nothing unusual when he had checked out the participants in Father O'Brian's literacy program. I wondered if we needed to back track his work there, too. Chief spit another piece of tobacco into the napkin and glowered at me. I knew he wasn't angry at me, personally, but was plenty ticked about the case in general, and our failure to turn up anything concrete, except for the footprint casts. He also didn't like conflict or confrontation. When I initially discovered this about his character I was surprised. Who would guess, looking at the big oaf, that he shied away from confrontation. His sheer size could intimidate the most contentious person to be agreeable. But, when he had to face a wayward employee and bring him back in line, it was the Chief, not the perpetrator, who was the most uncomfortable. I'm sure Rosini knew it. Everyone else at the office did.

On the other hand, Chief had compared me to a bulldog, noting that I never gave up, and once I was onto something or someone, he had a tough time getting me to let go. He was right, of course. I didn't mind confrontation at all. I didn't enjoy it, even with my worst enemy. But it was just part of the job. According to a personality inventory I had taken as part of one of my psychology classes in college, I was the type who could fire her best friend, if it became necessary. It wasn't one of the most flattering disclosures about my personality, but it was true.

I was sure it was best to leave Rosini to the Chief. We needed to focus our energy on the case, and not fragment ourselves with inner conflicts. But one day, Rosini and I would have to face-off and resolve our differences once and for all.

Chapter Thirteen

After a mere two hours of restless sleep, I woke in a rare bad mood. Even on my worse days, I usually managed to avoid sharing negative moods with people around me. Not today. I felt awful. An influx of hormones had brought water retention and irritability with it. I ordinarily overcame the hormonal roller coaster with my usual positive outlook on life.

Early autumn also brought with it a bumper crop of goldenrod and ragweed, two of my most irritating nemeses. So, add a sinus headache to PMS, then multiply by a factor of 10, the magnifier I associated with frustration over an unsolved case, with increasingly distant, cold leads. I couldn't let this one go unsolved. Griffin haunted me enough for a lifetime of cases.

I didn't bother to cover the dark circles beneath my eyes with makeup, since it would only accent their puffiness. With the summer sun only a memory, my hair was darkening to a drab, muted blonde, further robbing my face of what little color remained after exhaustion had drained most of it away. So, I wasn't interested in being a fashion plate or even attractive today! I dared anyone to comment!

I stomped into my office, flaunting the chip on my shoulder as I passed bewildered co-workers. Slamming my office door, I plopped down into my chair and glanced at the call waiting light. Anybody brave enough to call me today, had better have a very good reason to do so, or they would regret it! The intercom buzzed, and Sharon, my administrative assistant timidly announced that I had a visitor. I didn't want any visitors. Couldn't she send them away, at least until I'd had at least five or six cups of coffee?

Before Sharon could reply, I heard her say to someone else, "Sir, you can't just go in there." Then my door opened. Without turning around, I could guess who had pushed his way into my office. The annoying sniffling, with the nervous clearing of his throat, was almost a calling card for the ever-irritating Peales. Of all days for this aggravating twerp to come calling! I wondered what damage he had caused lately with his social media excursions. Maybe, just maybe, he had picked the perfect day to visit after all.

"Uh, Detect-t-tive Larsen," he stammered. I'd almost forgotten that he stuttered, too. Peales combined nearly every quality that yanked on my nerves. I had never had the pleasure of being around him during meals, but I could almost bet he chewed with his mouth open, and smacked his lips at the table. Today he had made two mistakes. One, by visiting me at all. Two, by chewing gum. True to my silent prediction, he smacked and popped it as he chewed. Add that to his habit of wiping his snotty nose with his bare hand, and you have just pushed me over the edge.

"What do you want?" I snapped. "And before you answer me, spit out that gum, use a Kleenex, and go wash your filthy, germy hands!" I commanded, tossing a box of Kleenex in his direction. He looked appropriately stunned, and I could tell I had hurt his feelings. Tough! Didn't parents teach their kids any manners anymore? I knew my immunity was probably at a record low, with my lack of sleep, poor nutrition, and high stress level. I didn't need to catch whatever made his nose produce its non-stop supply of mucous. He obediently blew his nose on a Kleenex, then looked in my direction. I pointed to the wastebasket, then led him to the door, and pointed to the men's restroom. "Wash them for a full minute with hot water and soap, and dry them thoroughly before you come back!" I commanded. He nodded and loped awkwardly off down the hall to comply.

I pulled out a package of disinfectant hand-wipes from my first aid kit and cleaned my door knobs before he returned. The slimy little germ-bag! What could he want, anyway? I was sure it was nothing I wanted to hear. Just as the disinfectant dried on the inner door handle, Peales timidly poked his head into my office, and I curtly motioned for him to come in. I might as well find out what he wanted, so he could leave, and leave me alone.

"O.K., out with it!" I barked.

"I, uh, feel real bad about all the t-trouble I caused you by putting my cousin's case on Facebook." He continued.

"You should feel bad, Mr. Peales." I snapped. "You interfered with a serious police investigation. It is possible that you gave information to some criminal who took that information and used it to commit the murder of Joanne Cavenaugh. I can't say for sure that you contributed to a murder. But, you obstructed justice in a big way. You are lucky you haven't been charged with criminal obstruction...yet." I let him digest that bit of information, and took a certain amount of pleasure in watching him flinch. I guess he thought his punishment was complete when he lost his job. That remained to be seen.

"Well, uh…. I wanted t-t-to make it up to you, Detective." That thought made me cringe. I hoped he wasn't trying to play detective again. "So, I made a Web page for the Cavenaugh murder and my cousin's murder, so fellow-s-s-urfers with any information could communicate leads…" He stopped mid-sentence when I grabbed my head in my hands, and dramatically laid it down on my desk. He looked at me like I had lost my sanity. I began to wonder how much more of this I could take before I did lose it.

"O.K., Peales, let's have what you came here to tell me." I lost all semblances of manners and patience. "And then, you are to close down your Web Page, and if you don't stop meddling in this case, I will go to court and get a restraining order to make you stop. Do you understand me?" I even surprised myself at how coldly and forcefully I delivered this ultimatum. My diction was almost staccato, as I emphasized each individual syllable.

He nodded and then reached into his pocket for a folded, wrinkled piece of computer printer paper. "Uh…Detective?"

"Yes, Peales, what is it?" I reached for the paper, but he drew back his hand, and didn't give it to me.

"I uh, wanted t-to-to t-talk t-to-to you before you see this lead because…"

I reached out and jerked the paper out of his hand. "Just give it to me and leave!" This time I got to my feet and shouted, while pointing to the door. He didn't move.

"You, uh..need t-t-to read it before I leave." He said with more backbone than I expected. O.K., anything to get him out of my office, out of my life.

I unfolded the paper and read it. Then I read it again. And again. It registered, but then it faded. No, my vision was fading. I couldn't have read it right. I glanced up and noticed Peales watching me. I had expected a sneer a la Rosini-style. But instead, Peales wore an expression of pity and concern.

"Are y-you all right, Detective?" He came over to my side of the desk and gave me an awkward pat on the shoulder. "I uh, w-wouldn't do anything t-to hurt you, I swear, Ma'am!"

The wind had been knocked from my very rude sails. "I know you wouldn't, Mr. Peales." I replied, quietly this time. "Now tell me what you know about this."

"Well, uh, Ma'am, I don't really know where to start. This l-l-lead was on my Web Page, of course. I don't know, uh, the sender, personally, but she has, uh, sent me messages before, you know, when I asked for advice, uh…before I c-called Texas to get a c-copy of my, uh…cousin's file." Hurry up! I said silently. My irritation was returning, along with the color to my face.

"Uh, the sender, and I don't even know her, uh, r-real name, uh, she says, like you have there, uh, that the Judge knew my cousin, and he was in Texas at the time of her murder. I, uh, checked with my mother, and it seems that Judge Beck, your fiancé, had dated another one of my older c-cousins, she's older than Sarah was, for a little while when they were in college. You know, uh… I was pretty young when Sarah was k-killed, so I uh, don't know much about it. I, uh, just know how much my m-mom cried about it, and uh, uhm, how angry my family was that you, uh….didn-n-n-t find who did it." He seemed to choke on the last sentence, and cast a very anxious look in my direction. After trying to comfort me with his awkward gestures, he had taken his seat again, and was looking me in the face as he delivered this information.

"My friend also says, as you c-can s-see, that the Judge, well he wasn't a judge then, had a little t-trouble with the law when he was in Texas. That's how, uh, she tracked down that he was uh, in Texas when my cousin was killed."

"Is there anything else, Mr. Peales?" I asked, my voice fading. "If not, would you please leave me alone to digest this information?" He nodded, then stood to leave. "Mr. Peales?" He turned to face me again. "Thank you for bringing this to me. I know it took a lot of courage. And please feel free to contact me if you find out anything else. Even though I was rude to you, I mean it when I say thanks. And, please accept my apology for being rude. I was having a bad day, and I don't feel well."

"That's O.K., Detective." He was more generous than I would have been in his place. " I imagine you feel even worse now. I'm s-sorry I had to bring uh, this uh, information to your attention." With that, he left me alone with my thoughts, and my pain.

I dialed Chief's number. He didn't bother hiding his concern. Since my legs were too weak to carry my body into his office, he was in mine within a minute. "Do I need to call the nurse?" he asked, anxiously pacing back and forth, trying to look in my eyes, and feeling the pulse in my wrist. Shaking my head, I weakly handed him Peales' Internet printout. His quick intake of breath betrayed his surprise, in spite of his efforts to remain calm. He looked as shaken as I felt.

Nathaniel, my Nathaniel. The man I thought was my soulmate. The only man I trusted. My hand flew to my throat. Nausea rose to my throat before it stopped short of vomiting. I had confided my innermost thoughts on this case to Nathaniel. I had told him about the bizarre non-sexual attack, with its sexual overtones, that had taken place while I slept. I hadn't even told Chief about that! What a fool I'd been! I had given my house key to only one person - the person I trusted most in life, the person I had planned on spending the rest of my life with. This time the nausea didn't stop. Dry heaves overcame me as I grabbed the trash can under my desk. I continued to analyze the situation, as the nausea worsened. Reluctantly I called Chief, and he rushed to my office, sensing something was terribly wrong.

Chief returned with a wet, cold paper towel as I finished depositing my morning coffee into the trash can. He had already asked Sharon to call housekeeping to come clean my office. I retreated to the ladies' room with the toothbrush and mouthwash.. He was nervously pacing when I returned. I shared with him what Peales had told me. Then I asked him to have a seat, because I had a lot more I needed to tell him.

When I finished telling Chief everything, he let out a low whistle. Reaching into his top shirt pocket for a cigar, he came back empty-handed. He hadn't anticipated a need to chew when he had rushed to my office earlier. Now he worked his jaw muscles without the cushioning of tobacco. I heard his teeth grinding against themselves as he started to talk, stopped, and then paced some more. Finally he stopped, blew out a big breath of air, then plopped into a chair across the desk from where I sat with my head down, resting my forehead in my hands. I had only cried once in Chief's presence. It had been a brief outburst, which I had stopped immediately. I knew he hated it, so today I did my best to stop before I started. I wasn't successful. The waterworks started, then continued, and continued and continued. I feared for a moment that I would vomit again, but at least that didn't happen.

Finally, Chief spoke, quietly, almost gently for such a rough-hewn giant of a man.

"Sam, I can't tell you right off what we are going to do about this. Obviously you have a big time conflict-of -interest with this lead. So, we'll take it one step at a time. I won't take you off the case. I trust you to continue with other aspects of the case, objectively, honestly, and thoroughly - all the things you are known for." I nodded. I believed with all my heart that a person's good name and honest reputation were more important than any personal relationship, even one that had, until yesterday, promised marriage. Ethics and honesty were primo for me. I wouldn't let myself or the Chief down - not anymore.

Chief wasn't finished. "As for the Judge, I'll handle that myself. You are not to have anything to do with it. Build that Chinese Wall, as they call it in legal circles. You are not to discuss any of this with the Judge, either. Not under any circumstances. I, in turn will be discreet, and will try not to ruin his reputation, unless he turns out to be guilty of something that precludes that." I knew Chief wasn't a grandstander. He hated the press as much as I did, so I didn't have to worry about him spilling anything that would harm Nathaniel. He would be fair, objective and thorough. That's all I could ask.

Of course, considering this tidbit of information had come from a Web page accessible by tens of thousands of people, I doubted that it would be kept quiet for very long. Chief understood the urgency of getting to Nathaniel before the press got wind of it, too. He called Nathaniel's chambers from my phone. "No, Judge," he said, with an unmistakable air of authority. "You need to cancel all of your appointments and all of your docket for the rest of the day. You'll agree with me that this is necessary after we talk. I advise you to get your tail over to my office right now, and don't stop to talk to anyone."

Turning to me, he commanded, "And you go home. Go to bed. Lock up real good, put on the alarm, don't answer the phone. I'll call you later. If you don't start feeling better by noon, you go to the doctor. That isn't a request, either. It's an order from your supervisor. Understand?" I understood. There was no place I would rather not be than the office when Nathaniel arrived. And there was nobody I would rather not talk to than him. I picked up my purse and headed out the door.

Chapter Fourteen

I hadn't thought sleep was possible. But, eventually physical needs overcome the emotional. I stumbled through my security check, but forced myself to be thorough and deliberate, as I checked and double-checked each lock, looked in each closet, behind each door, in the shower stall, under the bed. No more early morning surprises for me. I also had installed the extra deadbolt lock, and nobody but me had the key. I secured it, turned on the alarm system, then crashed. I enjoyed several hours of deep, dreamless sleep, or at least I didn't remember anything when I awoke.

I threw together a light snack around midnight. After washing it down with a glass of milk and brushing my teeth, I sank back into the comfort and security of my bed and went back to sleep until morning. When I woke up this time, I felt almost human. I flipped on a local morning news show for background noise while I ate breakfast and got ready to shower. I wasn't too surprised to hear the Internet message from Peales read over the airwaves. Any questions I had about my relationship with Nathaniel were answered in the prepared statement his administrator read to the media.

"State District Judge Nathaniel Beck expresses his confidence in the County law enforcement investigation, and further states that he is confident that he will be cleared of any and all suspicions regarding the murder of Sarah Griffin, eight years ago in Texas. While he admits to having had a casual dating relationship with Ms. Griffin's older cousin, and was in Texas at or near the time of Ms. Griffin's unfortunate and untimely death, the Judge denies unequivocally any involvement in or knowledge about her death, other than what was available to the general public through the news media.

Judge Beck regrets any inconvenience or embarrassment he may have brought to his office and the County Sheriff's office. He regrets to announce that his marriage to Detective Samantha Larsen will be temporarily delayed until the Sheriff's office completes its investigation of the allegations made against him, and that he reluctantly has decided to forego any social contact with his fiancé until that time as well, in order to avoid any appearance of impropriety or conflict-of-interest."

I was surprised to discover that the Chief had also issued a press statement on the subject. Apparently a great deal had hit the fan while I slept. The official County Sheriff's press release stated simply that Detective Samantha Larsen had voluntarily withdrawn from any part of the investigation of the Griffin and Cavenaugh murders that might involve Judge Beck, and that the Sheriff's office would initiate a total isolation of Detective Larsen from any and all matters pertaining to the Judge. Detective Larsen would, however, continue to investigate other aspects of the Cavenaugh murder which were determined by Chief Detective Sutton to be unrelated to the Judge. It added that Detective

Larsen agreed to a moratorium on any and all social contact with the Judge until investigation of his involvement concluded, and that she regretted as well that her marriage plans to the Judge would remain on hold until resolution of the issue.

I hadn't realized how much I had apparently talked in my sleep! I must have been quite articulate for it to translate so well for the press! Perhaps the next time the reporters cornered me on anything, I should ask them to wait until I was asleep, and I'd be happy to answer their questions. I personally would prefer handling the press that way.

Unwilling to venture outside for a run, I engaged in a few sit-ups and a few minutes of step aerobics before traipsing off to the shower. I stood in front of the mirror for what seemed like hours, watching the stranger with the sad green eyes. The empty hole where my heart had been a few days ago didn't look hollow in the mirror. Flesh and bones camouflaged the hollow spot very well. I was so used to the dark circles under my eyes, that they didn't seem unusual by now. But something was missing besides my heart. The spark that had lighted the emerald eyes was gone. The emeralds were dull and drab, no longer sparkling jewels that told stories of love and laughter and an adventuresome spirit. These eyes were old, wizened, and tired. Somewhere deep in the caverns reflecting the soul, was a pool of dark and foreboding hurt. To the casual observer, nothing had changed in my appearance since yesterday. In fact, I looked better this morning than I had immediately after my encounter with Peales and his crumpled Internet message. But to one experienced in reading the soul, to one who could see the heart, and know that mine was missing in action, I appeared wounded and heartsick.

I was a casualty of deceit and half-truths. Why had Nathaniel neglected to mention his connection to the Griffin family? Even though he and I hadn't known each other eight years ago, he knew without a doubt that I had been indirectly investigating that case to see if there was a connection to the

Cavenaugh murder. Doubts and suspicions swirled around in my mind, dancing with my imagination, and fueling my despair. Had it truly been an unplanned coincidence that we had met and started dating? Or had it been calculated, in case the Griffin case reopened at any time? Even worse, was it calculated by a serial killer who knew he might repeat his crime in the future? My instincts told me no, but I didn't trust them any longer.

Too bad I hadn't majored in Theater in college. I was going to need every ounce of self talk and acting talent I could muster. "O.K., let's practice, Sam", I muttered to myself. I would be both drama student and coach. "Step into that shower and give us a rendition of South Pacific. That's right. Now just a little louder. Shampoo with vigor while you sing." I got into the spirit of the charade, and belted out the only song I could think of that would fit my mood, "I'm gonna wash that man right out of my head, I'm gonna wash that man...." No, not so vigorously. Leave some scalp, and at least enough hair to cover it. That's better. Project your voice, but don't shout. Quality, quality. Loud doesn't necessarily equate with better."

I may not be a Streisand in the making, but singing in the shower was certainly therapeutic. No miracle cure, for sure. I knew it would take a long time and some positive answers to purge the twisted feeling inside my stomach. The hollow in my chest would take a long time to fill. But, I felt almost alive when I stepped out onto the bathroom rug. A little vigorous rubbing with a rough towel helped restore some of the circulation in my extremities that I felt sure I'd lost. They had alternated between cold and numb and back again throughout the morning.

A chill which could not be dispelled by any amount of warm clothing had settled into my joints. Like a wet, cold cloth, it sat there, penetrating deep into my core. As I stepped outside en route to my car, the cold, piercing wind drove it on icy fingers, deeper into my soul. But I trudged onward. Strapped my seatbelt, put the car in gear, and drove on auto pilot to the office.

I knew that nobody expected an exuberant, bubbly woman to emerge from the parking garage elevator. So, I didn't over compensate by pasting too bright a smile on my face. I decided that a thin, grim smile, with a nod and brief "Hello" would be appropriate. My inner drama coach Larsen drilled me for this performance as I parked my car and embarked on the day's adventures. "Head held high, but not too high, imagine that book on the top of your head, back straight, steady gaze, now walk... left, right, left, right, not too fast, loosen up those shoulders. O.K., turn the head slightly to your left, nod to Sharon. That's right, say 'good-morning'...good, even better than just 'Hello'. You're doing good. Just a few more steps. O.K. Now turn the door knob and enter your office, no not so fast, don't run. Deep breath, now try again, left, right, left, right. There. You've made it to your desk. Sit down...no, don't plop. Lower yourself slowly. They shouldn't hear your butt hit the leather out in the hall. There you go. Take another deep breath. Yes, your message light is blinking. But you don't have to answer it right away. Oh, very well. If you insist, you may pick up your messages. But don't hurry."

Could the casual observer tell that I was listening to an unseen coach as I went about my morning routine? I watched myself in my lipstick mirror for a while to make sure my lips weren't moving. Coach Larsen was darn good. I pulled off an award winning performance, and nobody was the wiser. I've been told that is the mark of a truly great performance. It looks natural, and the actor or actress is truly living the life of their character. I managed to stay in character as a calm, efficient law enforcement detective for most of the morning, slipping out of character only when my door was closed and I was alone with myself. Coach Larsen was on break, so I was able to let down my facade and momentarily droop into the heartbroken fiancé role.

Coach didn't take very long breaks, though, and she was quite a strict taskmaster. She had me whipped into character again in no time, and I finished the day tending to mundane paperwork that stacks up on a detective's desk during long weeks of an intense murder investigation. She forced me into an impromptu performance when Chief Sutton came to visit mid-afternoon. I'd studied my part, but hadn't had a chance to rehearse. He didn't seem to notice, sitting across the desk from me, chewing a soggy cigar, saying little. Said mostly he was just checking to see how I was doing, and congratulated me on holding together so well. He didn't know about Coach, and I didn't tell him. It didn't matter to him how I managed to get through the day, just so I did. He had been worried about me the day before. I could tell he still was a little worried, but also relieved that I didn't cry or throw up in front of him again. Coach said men didn't cope well with that type of behavior from females. I think she was right. Chief seemed to slow down his cigar chewing a bit as he talked about how things were going to turn out all right, and I would probably be back with the Judge before I knew it. No, he didn't know anything in particular that made him say that, and he reminded me even if he did, he wouldn't be able to discuss it with me. The Chinese Wall, remember. So, Coach said I should quit trying to read between the lines, and just let Chief do his job. I would know the outcome of the Chief's investigation in good time, and it wouldn't do me any good, mentally or physically to eat myself alive with worry.

Let me tell you, actresses and actors earn their money! So do directors and acting coaches. I was feeling the effects of strenuous exertion by the time I finally arrived back home. The phone rang as I dragged myself into my bedroom and began to change into some comfortable flannels. Although tempted to ignore it, I decided to take the adventuresome route and pick it up.

The voice mail message shouted from my phone when I picked it up. "Hey, Sam, sweetheart! I fully expected to talk to your machine." Dan's voice exuded his usual confidence and plentiful energy. "Go to a secure phone and call me back." That wasn't necessary today. The PI I'd hired to check for bugs had swept the house and checked my lines that afternoon. For once,

I could have an uncomplicated conversation with Dan without leaving home. So, he continued, "Your mom should have already left you a message on the machine. She wants you to come home for a few days, and so do I. There's some stuff I want to discuss with you in person, and she and I both think you need a break from the pressure cooker up there. The same news media that has made your life hell up there has brought all the news to us, too. So, we know what's been happening to you."

His suggestion sounded tempting. Besides, with my investigative activities curtailed, and my social life a standstill, I could probably take a couple of days off, bridge them with the weekend, and come back semi-refreshed.

"Hey, Sam, what's that computer kid up to, anyway?" Dan's question caught me off guard. My mind was already on vacation in Texas. I hoped Six Flags was still open on weekends. My kid brother, Alan, and I could ride the Texas Giant together. I could scream and scream, and nobody would know the scream had nothing to do with the roller coaster.

"What do you mean?" I asked. "Do you mean, what is he doing besides driving me nuts? Or what, technically, is he doing?"

"Well," he continued, "It seems that his little Web page of the two murders is generating a ton of so-called leads down here on the Griffin case. We've even had twenty or so nut cases confess. Pretty good recitation of details, too, considering they can read the whole file on the Net. We got one lead that we think is genuine, though. No confession, but good potential. Why don't you come on down and help out with it?" When I started to tell him I couldn't work on anything remotely tied to Nathaniel, he stopped me in mid-sentence. "I already know about that, Sam. Wouldn't have asked you down here if I thought any of this related to him in any way. Your Chinese Wall is intact."

That did it. I told Dan I'd be on either a red-eye or early morning flight to DFW. I'd call my mom after I made reservations.

Then I picked up the phone to tell the Chief. I was sure he would have no problem with it. In fact, I was sure he'd be relieved that I planned on getting some R & R to refresh my mind and recharge my inner battery. Besides, it was hunting season, and I knew he had no plans to work the weekend.

"Chief Sutton," he barked, with a slight smile in his voice. I could hear other masculine voices in the background.

"Are you having a party, Chief?"

"Nah, just some of the guys stopped in to see who was going to bag the biggest game this weekend," he replied. "Yah, go on, go ahead for a few days. Nothin' happening on any part of the case you're allowed to work on, anyway."

"What on earth is that sound?" In the background, I could hear a grating noise, like fingernails on a chalkboard that made the hair stand up on my neck and arms.

"Oh, that. Nothin' really. Rosini's in here showing us some do-dad that he's started making, in addition to his hunting calls. Says he's going to retire on the money he gets from it. Seems the farmers around here use it like a pest repellent. Sounds like a screech owl or something, that furry critters don't take to. He's got his own web page now for his little business and has ads in *Field and Stream* and *Progressive Farmer.* He thinks he's going to be richer than any of us. Probably will be, with our luck. Work twenty years and make more with little bird calls and obnoxious noises than you did as a Cop. That's the way life is, all right."

Chief seldom talked for more than a couple of syllables without spitting and chewing. Today he sounded relaxed and talkative. I guess the prospect of a weekend out with the boys had loosened his tongue. Or maybe he was just nervous talking to me, or relieved that I wasn't there in person to embarrass him. It didn't matter. He gave me permission to go home. I needed the trip. I needed to be home, to be nurtured and secure. I hung up and made my airline reservations.

Chapter Fifteen

I expected to see my mother when I stepped off the plane in DFW airport the next morning. Dan surprised me, instead. "Thought we could talk while I drive you to your folks' place," he explained, as he steered me towards the baggage claims turnstile. I assure you my car is not bugged, so we can talk candidly."

I waited at the curb while he brought his car around. I'd packed light, but still didn't feel like walking in the stifling heat. It had been 50 degrees when I left the Iowa municipal airport. It was already 85 and muggy here. An unseasonal heat wave had settled in for several days. I'd forgotten how it could sap my strength.

We didn't talk while Dan navigated the traffic snarls getting out of the airport. But once out on LBJ Freeway, he started filling me in on what he wanted to discuss, before we got to my parent's house. It seems he had two motives for asking me to come to Texas. One was personal, and the other business.

"Where are we going?" I asked, as he made an unexpected turn-off from the usual route to my parents' house.

"I need to concentrate on what I'm saying, and can't with all this traffic." he explained. As usual, the loop was a mix between a race track and a parking lot. I understood completely, or so I thought. As soon as he pulled into a strip shopping center in Irving, I wasn't so sure.

"Uh, Sam, I think I'd better get the personal issue out of the way, first," he said, as he took my hand. Even after all these years, my flesh burned when he touched it. I could tell he experienced a similar response, and he didn't like it any more than I did. "I'm seeing someone pretty seriously right now," he continued." I plan to ask Debbie to marry me, but I want to make sure I can make a commitment that I can be proud to make. I mean, I know I love her, but do I love her enough? I still love you, too, Sam. I needed to see you in person to know if I loved you too much to make a proper commitment to Deb. Do you understand?"

I understood more than he knew. I'd struggled with the same issue when I said I'd marry Nathaniel. "Dan, you know we will love each other probably the rest of our lives," I was telling the truth, even though I often tried to ignore it. "But, you know our love isn't one that works. I just don't think that kind of intense passion was meant for marriage. A once-in-a lifetime kind of fire, but not the kind that takes you into old age together." He nodded in agreement. "I do wish it was different." I looked into his face and saw the same old smoldering flame reflected in his eyes. The slightly dilated pupils, surrounded by the deepening azure blue, probably mirrored my own involuntary physiological changes. I knew only too well what was on his mind, because my own thoughts had taken a detour, too.

"You know we shouldn't," I mumbled, as he reached across the arm rest that separated us, and touched his lips to mine. I was reminded of a sad old priest, who described this kind of passion that had consumed him many years ago, and had created the daughter he loved so much, but could never publicly claim. My mind didn't linger on the practical, or the murder case, or anything it should have focused on, though. I don't know how many minutes our kiss lasted. I wasn't even sure if I breathed from the time I felt Dan's firm, but soft lips press down on mine, or when I melted into his mouth and savored the taste I had missed for so many years, without being aware that I had missed it. When we finally parted, breathless, with pulses racing, we both knew we could not repeat it, no matter how much the magnets in our bodies and souls drew us together.

"You know that needs to be an official farewell kiss, don't you?" I asked the question neither of us wanted to answer. My romantic future with Nathaniel was in limbo, but I didn't want anything to stand in the way of Dan's happiness.

It didn't take long for us to fall back into our old habits of reading each other's thoughts. "You know, everything is going to work out for you and the Judge," he said.

He continued, " I'm not just saying empty words that are nice to hear. When I say I know it, I mean I know it, O.K.?" Now, that brings me to the business part of asking you down here. We've had a solid lead in the Griffin case after all these years. I'm pretty sure it's genuine, and I'm confident we are going to crack it this time. So, I wanted you down here when we did. You need to be a part of it."

I nearly shouted with excitement, "What kind of lead could surface after all these years... and don't tell me it has something to do with that irritating little Geek and his Internet meddling," I could feel my blood pressure rising, just thinking of all the complications Peales had created.

It seems that someone with a conscience had come forward. One of Sarah Griffin's married undergraduate professors from UT Arlington, with whom she had an affair, was now terminally ill with a brain tumor. He had been spurred to come forward by all of the publicity that had surrounded the Cavenaugh case and its possible ties to the Griffin case. When he read about the Judge's possible connection with Griffin's he couldn't sit by and allow an innocent man to endure prosecution which he didn't deserve. The professor also wanted to make peace with God and right a wrong he had allowed to continue for too many years."

No, the professor hadn't killed Sarah Griffin, but he had his suspicions about who did. Not wanting his relationship to be disclosed after Sarah's death, he had kept quiet, and the knowledge which could crack this case, remained hidden. He was tempted after his divorce two years ago to come forward, but it wasn't until recently when he stared his own mortality in the face, that he felt guilt-ridden enough to finally do what was right.

The leads were cold, and so far Dan and his fellow detectives had been unable to chase down the people involved. But they more plausible than anything we'd had to work with eight years earlier. At the time of her death, having just finished her pre-nursing requirements, Sarah Griffin had started classes at nursing school. The nursing school was located just down the street from the County hospital, where her body had been dumped. She worked a few hours a week at the hospital as a nurse's aide to make a little spending money, and to gain experience helpful to her nursing duties. According to the professor, Sarah had told him about one of her classmates who worried her. It seems the classmate also worked part time at the same hospital, and had somehow managed to get involved in a narcotics supply line.. The classmate and her boyfriend marketed the drugs, while the other members of the team obtained them by manipulating doses given to patients, so the shortages were never noticed on shift change narcotics counts. Sarah was not part of the ring, but had discovered it, and had confronted the classmate, threatening to go to the police. The rest is history. She hadn't lived long enough to follow-through with her plans.

Sarah had not been raped. The professor confessed to having had consensual sex with her within a few short hours before her murder. This information, alone shot numerous holes through the theory of a serial killer having murdered Joanne Cavenaugh. But it wasn't known to anyone but the professor. Now it became urgent to locate the former classmate and the boyfriend. Dan had obtained the nursing school's class rosters for the year Sarah was killed. They had already sent a detective to Austin to compare the roster to records at the State Board or Nurse Examiners, to track down all members who had eventually taken Board exams. Those students would be the easy ones to track down, since the Board's records contained married names, current addresses, and out-of-state records on those who had moved and sought license reciprocity in their new states. The tough ones would be those who hadn't make it through nursing school. Dan had saved those for me to investigate.

My curiosity whetted, and my investigator's instincts on high alert, I was ready to start right away. But, Dan turned the key in the ignition and drove me to my parents, instead. I accepted his invitation to dinner to meet Debbie the next evening. In spite of the Texas heat, I felt invigorated. It was a pleasant change from the droopy, exhausted person I had left behind in Iowa. Some days I wondered if I had made a mistake moving so far away from home. Then I touched my lips and remembered the fire that still lingered from Dan's kiss, and I knew I had made the only choice that made any sense.

Mom got appropriately weepy and sentimental when I walked in the front door. But I have to admit, it felt good to have her arms around me, and the warm, soft feeling of her cheeks against mine. Dad grabbed me in a bear hug, as mom returned to the kitchen, where tantalizing aromas of my favorite home-cooked foods wafted from the oven. I detected a subtle hint of bay leaf, intermingled with the unmistakable smell of roast beef smothered in onions. Dormant saliva glands snapped to attention, tweaked to life by my underused sense of smell which had now also revived with gusto. I knew the roast was also flanked by new potatoes and baby carrots. I would have known, even without the dusting of wheat flour on mom's apron that she was kneading dough for bread, Soon the sweet, pungent aroma of cinnamon and peaches would join the blend of cooking potpourri that told my senses I was home. Home, sweet home. How I had missed my loved ones, the food and pleasantries we had converted to family traditions through years of loving rituals.

A recent school picture of my kid brother, Alan smiled at me from where it rested on top of the piano. In my mind he was still eight years old, frozen in time when I had left home to seek my investigative fortunes up north (as my mom called it). But, that smile, which had progressed through the years, through transient toothlessness of elementary school, now sported metal brackets of middle school orthodontia. I couldn't believe he was on the threshold of adolescence. Alan was not just mom's change-of-life baby. He had been her last egg, one last surprise before menopause. We were nearly sixteen years apart. The big age difference between us had more than once caused strangers in the mall or distant relatives to mistake him for my own child. For my parents, it was almost like raising two separate families. While I danced the night away at my homecoming dance, they stayed home and changed diapers. While I studied for college entrance and SAT exams, Alan learned toilet training. But, when I went away to start a new life in the Midwest, they were spared the agonies of the empty nest syndrome.

I know my parents wanted me to settle down and start a family of my own. But, they were keenly aware of my most recent pain in that regard, and diplomatically avoided the subject altogether. Dan deposited my luggage in the guest bedroom, which had been my room when I lived at home. He encircled my waist with his strong, protective arms, giving me a parting hug. "See you tomorrow night," he whispered, as he grazed my cheek with a warm, platonic kiss. Our eyes held for a second too long, as I read the latent passion in their depths, which reflected my own, like a mirror to the soul.

"One quick question, before you leave," I implored, reluctant to see him go. "Is this relationship with Debbie as consuming as ours was?" He knew what I meant. We had consumed each other with our passion. You might think that was good. We initially thought that passionate people should bond with similar passion. But, there was no balance. We both approached life with equal measures of passion. But there was no space for rest or distance to recuperate from passion that scorched each other with its intensity. We could never get enough passion from the other or give enough passion to the other. The only conclusion to such unbridled living was burn-out, and we had suffered burn-out as passionately as we had created it. Dan and I both knew that we could never work as a couple. We also knew we could never resist being a couple if we maintained close proximity to each other.

"No, Sam, it isn't as passionate as us," he broke through my musing. "We both know that isn't possible. But, we have compatibility, and I need that. I'm ready to settle down to a comfortable life that will take me into old age with someone - and not push me into old age prematurely!" Although he grinned when he said the last remark, I knew he was serious. Just as I was with my relationship with Nathaniel. Neither of us could afford to pursue what might have been. We knew what that was, and what it would be again, if we didn't confine ourselves to a platonically appropriate relationship. I'm sure he experienced the same twinges of possessive jealousy about Nathaniel as I did about his Debbie. But the rational part of each of us was happy that the other had found someone to love, someone to settle down with, to have a home and family. Our passion for each other would always lurk just beneath the surface, but we wouldn't allow it to interfere with our futures.

"I look forward to meeting her tomorrow, then," I smiled. "She's a lucky girl, and if you love her, then I'm sure she is very special." I was proud of myself for being so magnanimous.

"Yeah, I have great taste," he grinned somewhat sadly. "I love only the best women in the world, you know." Then he turned and left before either of us could say anything more, or before one of us could find an excuse to touch the other, to linger, to allow our senses to reminisce.

"Tomorrow then," I called after him, as he quietly shut my door and left me there alone.

Chapter Sixteen

I dressed more carefully for dinner with Dan and Debbie than I had for most of my dates with Nathaniel. I confess to being more nervous, too. I wondered if the two of them were nervous. Dan hadn't asked Debbie to marry him yet, so I reminded myself to be careful and not let that tidbit of information slip during our conversation. Just what did an ex-wife say when dining with a future wife, especially when both of them loved the man in their own special way?

Did I dare let Debbie know that I still loved Dan? I'm sure it would show in a million little ways, in every nuance, every stolen glance, every tiny tip of flame still smoldering in our eyes, behind the carefully controlled facade of distance. I wanted Dan to be happy, and I sincerely hoped Debbie was the woman who could help him get there. But a part of me was sad, mourning for what could never be, yet reveling in the memories of what was.

My complexion had taken on a healthy pink glow which had been absent for several weeks before coming back to Texas. On the surface, I credited a day spent with Alan at Six Flags, chapping somewhat in the wind as we rode every daring ride in the park. I'm sure the increased blood flow from the G-force levels on the Cliff Hanger and Flash Back contributed, and let's not forget the benefits of loud screaming on those rides. I felt younger than I had in months. But, I couldn't stay in a borrowed teenage time warp forever.

A fleeting, momentary prodding from my evil, mischievous alter-ego almost talked me into wearing the daring red dress I'd worn on my last date with Nathaniel, but I decided to present a more dignified, less flamboyant ex-wife image than that, at least for the first meeting with Debbie.

Dan had called to find out my dining preference, and had initially suggested a bland, neutral feeding ground.. While I loved their "down home cooking", and had agreed that everything on their menus was excellent, I reminded him that I'd enjoyed my share of "down home" cooking, and that I could get plenty of Mom's meatloaf or chicken fried chicken with mashed potatoes and cream gravy up in Iowa. What I couldn't get was good, authentic Tex-Mex that would burn out the roof of your mouth on a good day. It had been too long since my tongue had suffered blissful agony from the scorching onslaught of pico de gallo, or reveled in a perfect blend of cumin, chilies and cilantro, or the fresh sizzle of genuine fajitas. I'd had to resort once to a frozen diet fajita dish when the craving hit, and had been as let down as one could be when the soggy, pasty tortilla surrounding a pre-cooked, tasteless slab of meat, had fallen far short of the real article. No, I would not settle for bland tonight. If we couldn't have Mexican fare, then Cajun would be my second choice. Iowa Blue Gill was delicious and delicate, but didn't quite satisfy a craving for deep fried alligator, or a bowl of thick, steaming gumbo.

I wondered silently if Debbie was too bland to tolerate either cuisine. Somehow I knew that she would graciously go along with whatever I chose, just to please Dan. It made me happy yet sad at the same time. Maybe our relationship would have worked better or longer if I had subrogated my personality to please Dan. But he didn't want that, and neither did I. It was my passionate nature that drew him to me, and his that drew me to him. Neither of us would have tolerated a counterfeit substitute. If Debbie was able to make such a compromise naturally, or if her personality allowed it to be a spontaneous reaction which made her happy, too, then it would work for them. I hoped that was the case.

I opted for the conservative emerald green sheath I'd bought at the mall before embarking on my day of frivolous fun at the amusement park. It nearly matched my eyes, which had recaptured their lost sparkle, even though a hint of sadness lingered in the clandestine recesses, visible only to the most observant. Something in Texas definitely agreed with me. Achieving truly restful sleep, and submerging myself in the sanctuary of family cohesiveness had erased the ever-present dark circles, which had ringed the emerald pools in days of recent past. Some unseen eraser had swooped down out of nowhere and touched other parts of my face, bringing me back from the premature lines which had etched the corners of my mouth and eyes just one week earlier.

The gaunt hollows of my cheeks, although fashionable, had created a Kate Moss image only days earlier. Now, the healthy plumping of a couple of pounds and relaxation of the underlying muscles, replaced the gaunt look, and gave me back the healthy, all-American girl look that was really me. When I smiled at myself in the mirror, it traveled all the way to my eyes, and replaced the forced expression I'd substituted for a smile during the weeks of the Cavenaugh murder investigation.

By the time Dan and Debbie arrived, I once again resembled the uncomplicated, pleasant, yet no-nonsense Sam Larsen who had grown up in Texas, when my home town was still a small bedroom community for the metroplex. Now it was a booming metropolitan area of its own, riddled with a rash of violent crimes over the past few years that had stunned long-time residents and transient student residents alike. The kidnapping and murder of a young girl who had been riding her bike in the middle of the day near her grandparent's home, had stunned a nation, and frustrated local and federal law enforcement agencies when no perpetrator was brought to justice. Take it from me, though, it was never too late to solve a crime. Solving the Griffin case should give other crime victims and the police hope for an eventual arrest in other cold cases, even after the task forces assigned to their investigations were disbanded. I only hoped the pervert who had killed the child hadn't had a chance to harm another one before he slipped up, or someone who knew the truth came forward, allowing him to be caught.

I promised myself and Dan that we would not talk cop shop. The night belonged to him and Debbie. I was determined to honor that pledge, and to make the evening as pleasant as I could for both of them. I wondered if Debbie was as nervous about meeting me as I was about meeting her.

The doorbell rang and Dan appeared to escort me to his car. He introduced the lovely brunette in the front seat, and we shook hands. I would have the luxury of studying her from the back seat on the way to the restaurant. The two of them held hands, and I sensed an aura of quiet confidence in her personality and her relationship with Dan. Debbie continued to display good taste and decorum after we were seated in the restaurant. I noticed she avoided the spicier entrees, opting for chicken fried steak instead of true south-of-the-border cuisine, but she never commented about not liking Mexican food, and never made it an issue. If I could sum up her personality with one word it would have to be "gracious." But she was significantly more than gracious. I dare not portray her as too bland, because plain vanilla she was not. As a legal secretary to a partner in one of the big multinational law firms, she was accustomed to compromising and making it look natural. Her boss was notorious for his flamboyant and volatile personality. She undoubtedly offered stability and the only tranquility available to that professional match. At the same time, I detected an inner strength that quietly asserted itself as necessary. While outwardly easy-going, I knew there was a toughness that had allowed her to survive in the shark pit of modern law firms.

Dan would be inheriting a ready-made family, too. Debbie proudly displayed a photo of a cute, freckle-faced eight-year-old boy, with hazel eyes and dark brown hair to match her own. Now I understood where she had gained her inner toughness and strength. She had learned it as a single parent. I had determined to make the most of the evening, and to concentrate on being cordial and friendly. As the evening progressed, however, I found myself genuinely enjoying the company, and genuinely liking this young woman who was destined to be my beloved Dan's new wife. He had chosen well.

I expected to receive appropriately tasteful Christmas cards with family pictures of a handsome detective and his lovely wife and children for many years to come. And, if I kept in touch, I could expect an invitation to their home for dinner whenever I was in the neighborhood. Sort of like an aunt who lived out of town, but who got along well with the family and was welcomed when she visited. But one who wouldn't live near enough to become a daily presence in their lives. I was pretty sure I could live with that. And I knew I could always count on Dan to be there for me if, like Cavenaugh, I encountered a difficult case and needed a trusted professional to help me solve it.

By the time the sopapillas arrived we could pass for three old friends who had met for an evening of reminiscing about old times. The two of us who could have talked about the old times, didn't. We all concentrated on making new memories for the moment and for the future. I lifted my margarita slightly, and proposed a pretty nice toast, "To my friends, Dan and Debbie. God smile on your love, and bless you with much happiness. And may we stay friends for all times. Always,." Well, maybe I'd tried too hard to catch up on all the margaritas I'd missed while in Iowa. The "always" sounded a little sappy and a little slurred. I drank very little, and had little tolerance for alcohol, so even one margarita would have created this effect. I hadn't stopped at one. Dan knew me too well. I didn't often become lubricated with booze, and the only other time I'd had more than one drink in his presence, he'd had to carry me into the house. He called for the check, and suggested we stop for a cup of coffee on the way home, so he didn't have to do the same tonight.

As he helped me out of the car once we arrived at my parent's home, I surprised myself and reached forward to say goodbye Debbie. The handshake that started as friendly, but distant, just wouldn't do.. I squeezed her hands instead, and gave her a brief, but sincere embrace. "I really meant that toast," I told her. "And if you like, I'll repeat it when I'm one hundred percent sober."

Chapter Seventeen

I felt a bit guilty going to church the next morning with my parents and a slight hangover. Not a raging headache, or intolerance for noise as I remember having experienced once or twice in my late teens when experimentation had been my lot. I was a boring teenager, actually. My rebellion was pretty subdued. I tried to smoke once or twice, but couldn't stand the taste of cigarettes, and hated the way they made my throat feel. I felt about the same way about alcohol. For the most part I couldn't stand the way it tasted. Mom occasionally used an aromatic spirit in some of her recipes. I liked certain coffees with a little spirited lacing. I liked an occasional margarita on a hot night. I think I liked the mixers more than I liked the liquors, though.

Even with a slight hangover, I felt better than I had in weeks, if you subtract the two days and two nights since I had come home. I tried to go to church on at least a semi-regular basis in Iowa, but it was difficult to keep a regular schedule when my own schedule was so erratic. It was very different going to worship, sitting next to family, than it was sitting by myself on a pew near the back of the church. Same God, same message, but a lot warmer and more fulfilling sitting there with mom and dad. Alan chose to sit with his buddies, but they all sat near the front of the sanctuary, so all of the parents had a ready view of their activities.

I was pretty proud of my brother for acting so grown up and serious in church. He seemed to be growing into a fine young man, with a great deal of social sensibility and responsibility. I'd seen many kids who had been born to older parents who were not so responsible. The parents seemed to be too tired from having raised other children, or just excused themselves for being older, to take an active role in raising the last child. Often that youngest child was spoiled by older siblings. My career had prevented that from happening. I had always impressed upon Alan how important it was for him to not turn out like some of the young people I had encountered as a street cop. I gave my parents full credit, though, for the fine young man he was becoming. They hadn't spared him any of the value lessons I had received, and there was no difference between the behavior they expected from him and what they had expected from me. If he disobeyed, they meted out the same punishment they had meted out to me. So, all in all, they had raised two very responsible, dynamic offspring.

After church we went out to a restaurant for a family dinner. Mom had knocked herself out cooking all of my favorites since I arrived. I wanted her to relax and be waited on at least once. We talked about family stuff. I don't even remember the various topics of conversation. Mostly small talk about who was doing what, news from distant relatives, the sort of bantering that keeps a family connected. I had missed this type of conversation, and promised myself I'd find a way to work it into my life once I returned to Iowa. There was no doubt in my mind that I would go back to the Midwest. I couldn't stay here, near Dan. Even with him married to someone else, we still needed our distance.

I would find a way to take the time to be less intense and less serious in my personal life when I got back to Iowa. Why couldn't I call it home, yet? I already knew the answer to that question. Once we finally solved the Griffin murder case, I could get back with Nathaniel. No more delaying our marriage. I needed a home base, with a solid partner. Maybe start a family. Well, I wasn't in too much of a hurry for a family. I had a few years before my biological clock started audibly ticking. I hoped by then to be happily, solidly married to a stable man, with whom to start a family.

Sunday faded uneventfully into nightfall. I excused myself from family activities and withdrew to my room. Mom hadn't changed the room much when she converted it into a guest room. The biggest change was in name only. It was still my room, with all of my paraphernalia intact. For the most part, I was the only guest who stayed in this room. So, retreating to my room was like slipping into a comfortable haven, one where I could always think clearly and decisively. Tonight was no different from when I had retreated into this room as a teenager. Except, I had much more sophisticated and serious homework to study than I had back then.

The next morning, I would begin my interviews with the former nursing students who hadn't finished their studies or gone on to become registered nurses. I suspected that the woman we were looking for was part of the group assigned to me. I couldn't imagine anyone being cold and callused enough to enter into a profession known for its caring and giving nature, after witnessing or participating in a brutal murder of her classmate.

Monday morning bright and early I began my quest. I had only ten contacts to make. The first two were quite easy. I had tracked these women fairly quickly through marriage records. Four of the ten had been married multiple times, so I had a little extra work to find their current names and locations. The first three on my list reported quitting nursing school to get married. One woman was now an elementary school teacher, having chosen that profession in order to have more time with her family. The second young woman had married the doctor she had been dating at the time she quit school. Their marriage was a solid one, and she was happily a homemaker and stay-at-home mother, in a well-to-do neighborhood.. She was active in PTA, scouting, and band boosters. I hadn't thought of Rosini since arriving in Texas. But meeting this young woman made me think about him. She surely must be the role model for his idea of the perfect woman.

One had stayed in the medical field, but had switched her field to Physical Therapy. She was so busy, working for a home health agency, that had difficulty meeting up with her. Each woman reviewed my list of names, and offered information on several with whom they had run into occasionally through the years. By the time I had completed my third interview, I had a pretty good idea which two names on my list held the answer to my mystery.

All three women independently described Angela Wright as a troubled young woman, who didn't take school seriously, and who hung around young men who seemed to have a dark side. They all wondered why she had chosen nursing as a course of study. I theorized, but didn't tell them, that I suspected it was so she would have ready access to narcotics.

I found Angela at home at her dingy, tiny one bedroom apartment, with her most current boyfriend, a tough looking man, with the classic dental decay of meth mouth. The smell of stale tobacco permeated the filthy apartment, and it was obvious I had interrupted more than sleep when I knocked on the door.

I had called Dan before approaching the front door. The apartment complex itself was a picture of decay and neglect, with plywood and foil covering broken windows. Mangy cats rummaged through scattered trash that littered the grounds. The whole place smelled musty and was covered with an infection of mildew. I had no desire to become a victim, myself. I had no delusions of grandeur, and no unmet needs to become a hero. I just wanted to find the truth, and let the truth liberate all of us who had invested our hearts and souls in finding who had killed Sarah Griffin. My heart was probably more invested than the others.

Angela was a picture of neglect and hard living. Her stringy, shoulder length brown hair had been dyed a harsh red sometime in the past. Two toned, greasy strands hung in clumps around a puffy, pitted face, with equally puffy eyelids that nearly obscured her bloodshot pale, blue eyes. She too, had large cavities in one of her front teeth. She reeked of stale tobacco, and yellow nicotine stains painted her hands. Like her boyfriend, she had decorated her body with an assortment of tastelessly placed tattoos. She yawned in my face, and offered me a stale cup of coffee from a dirty, stained mug. I declined. She explained that she needed some coffee since she waited tables in an all-night bar and hadn't yet been to sleep.

Dan arrived. With his commanding presence, we didn't have any trouble convincing the boyfriend to leave, so we could talk to Angela alone. She looked like a stray animal that had been running loose on its own for too long, and was almost relieved to be caught. When I first laid eyes on Angela I had anticipated a very long, possibly unproductive interview with her. But something in her eyes said otherwise. She looked like a person possessed by a tormentor.

It didn't take a lot of persuasion to convince Angela to open up to us. She acted as though she had been waiting for this moment for years. Eight years to be exact. Dan, sensing that she was about to disclose some pretty incriminating information, gave her a rendition of her Miranda rights, which she waived.

"I just want to get this out," she sighed, wearily. Slumping into a faded, stained and threadbare armchair, she took a deep breath and continued. "I'm the person you're talking about. I was in on the narcotics ring, along with my boyfriend. It was his idea for me to go to nursing school. I didn't like any of it. I hated the sight of blood, and didn't want to clean up nobody's mess, if you know what I mean. Didn't really plan to get involved in nothin', really. I didn't know Duke was in on anything, either. I just wanted some fun, a little booze, a joint now and then. But, he got me mixed up with them before I knew it. I liked the stuff, but he wouldn't let me have any of it unless I helped get my hands on it. So, he put me in touch with a couple of nurses and one resident doctor who knew how to fix up the patient's charts, and give them just half a dose of their pain pills, pocketing the other half. It was a pretty good racket. We all made a lot of money, and sometimes took our pay in dope, if we felt like it."

"Then that nosy, holier-than-thou Griffin chick accidentally caught one of the nurses one night. I didn't know she was in the room, cleaning up the roommate to the one whose med's we were keeping. So I busted in to take the extra pill out of the nurse's pocket, so she wouldn't get caught, and Sarah caught us both. She threatened to tell on us. We couldn't let her do that. The nurse just wanted to give her a shot of something, but she ran from us. I called Duke and told him what was goin' on. He waited in the parking garage when she got off, and you know the rest. He choked her to death with a leather strap he cut off a horse whip he kept in his house. Yeah, we played with whips and stuff sometimes when we was high. I liked it, made the sex better sometimes, especially when I couldn't remember nothin' the next day."

"I didn't know Duke was going to kill her, honest. He threatened to kill me, too, if I told anyone. And I knew he meant it, so I shut up. Then, after he was killed in a motorcycle accident a couple of years ago, I thought about coming forward, but figured it was too late. So, I just shut up and went on with life, as you can see, it ain't much of a life, but that's what I ended up with."

I left it up to Dan to decide if she should be arrested as an accomplice or for obstruction of justice. He told her she would need to go to the station to give a complete statement, and his superior would make the decision.

"I don't care anymore, anyway it goes," she sighed, and got up to put on some street clothes. "I'm just glad it's over. I haven't had much of a life since then, as you can see. I'm just real tired." Dan nodded, and then motioned for me to accompany her while she got dressed, just in case she had any suicidal ideation.

I accompanied Dan and Angela to the police substation where all of the loose ends were tied up on the Griffin case after nearly a decade. We made sure that newspapers in Texas and Iowa got the story in time for front page headlines the next morning. I picked up a copy to read on the plane ride back to Iowa.

Dan drove me to the airport, and we said another, bittersweet, good-bye, this time just a hug. A chapter in our lives had finally concluded. I felt an inner peace that had eluded me for so many years. I had accomplished a lot on this short, four day trip. Both the Griffin case and my relationship with Dan had lacked closure when I left Texas for Iowa six years ago. Now I had satisfactory closure with both of them. It was time to reclaim my life in Iowa, and start making memories of my own.

We didn't need to put our feelings into words. Dan and I both knew we would share a special, but unworkable love for our lifetimes. We both wished each other well in our new lives, and deeply regretted that it could never work between us. We both looked forward to the happiness we knew awaited us with our other loves, the ones we both planned to make last a lifetime.

My parents had bid me tearful good-byes at the house. Alan had shared breakfast with me before going off to school, and had planted an awkward, brotherly kiss on my cheek, as I gave him a sisterly squeeze. I'd admonished him to keep up the good work. He was a good kid, and I didn't want to hear that he had changed. I think he took my threat to come back to kick his butt in person if he strayed quite seriously.

I had to go find closure on two fronts in Iowa. I needed to reaffirm my relationship with Nathaniel, if indeed that was possible. I wondered how I could have doubted him in the first place. I worried that it meant I didn't trust him or know him as well as I once thought. Fortunately, Chief had precluded any communications between Nathaniel and me, and I had never had the chance to voice my doubts to him in person. So, he didn't know about them.

Now, I had to figure out who our copy-cat killer was. After finding out the truth about Sarah Griffin's murder, there was no doubt that the Cavenaugh murder was an imitation of it. I resolved to solve it in short order.

Chapter Eighteen

Chief Sutton met my flight, and we spent the next hour driving around, catching up on what had happened in Iowa, as well as what had happened in Texas when the Griffin story hit the papers. He said Rosini had been in to see him with another idea on how to solve the Cavenaugh case. I was doubly eager to solve the case, foremost, so justice could be done. But I was no less interested in concluding the case so I could be done with Rosini. I never wanted to work on another case with him.

Before we became too engrossed in Rosini's idea I wanted to find out if there had been any news from Nathaniel. Chief had personally contacted Nathaniel as soon as I had called from Texas to inform him that the Griffin case had been finally solved. I asked if Nathaniel had said anything indicating where our future stood. Chief grinned, then spit his tobacco out the car window before responding. He said, "The judge expressed relief and gratitude that his name had been cleared, and unofficially told me that he planned to make it up to you."

He continued, after spitting some more tobacco juice into the wind, "He knows I'm collecting you at the airport, and asked me to tell you he would call you later today after you got settled in, and he never doubted that you knew him well enough to know he'd never kill anyone. And, by the way. I personally investigated the so-called trouble he was in down in Texas at the time the Griffin girl was killed. You know, the supposed lead that tipped off Peales' internet friend. Well, as it turns out, the Judge was with some old college buddies, and some of them were drinking and laughing too loud at a public bar, where they'd gone to celebrate old times. The whole bunch of them got in trouble when someone complained, and they were all charged with being drunk and disorderly. Your man was guilty only by association, and when he insisted on getting a blood alcohol level run on himself, it proved he was well below the legal level, not drunk by any long shot. So, he didn't really have a personality change from the man you know today. Same guy; conservative, law-abiding, good material for a future politician and family man. For what it's worth, you still have my blessing for a marriage to the guy." I was relieved to know that my instincts about Nathaniel were on point. I still hoped the instincts about Rosini were wrong.

Well, time to hear about Rosini's idea. Chief told me Rosini had theorized that whoever killed Joanne must have seen her coming and going at the hospital, and for whatever reason, had followed her home the night she was killed. So, he thought we should do a stake-out around the hospital to see if we could come up with any leads, or maybe catch the person who killed her. I had to admit, it was a plausible theory. We had no other evidence to contradict it, and it was worth a try. I surprised the Chief by agreeing to it. He suggested that I tell Rosini in person that I agreed with him. Chief also wanted me to team up with

Rosini for this part of the investigation, so we could both share in the credit if it worked out, and resulted in catching the killer.

Rosini was waiting for us in Chief's office when we arrived at the station. I had dropped off my luggage at home, and looked around to make sure nothing was amiss beforehand. We decided to start our stake-out that very night, so I begged off for the afternoon to talk to Nathaniel and to get a nap.

Before I left the station, I went to my office to pick up mail and messages. A very excited and urgent message from Harry in forensics awaited me on voice mail. He had delivered it just moments before. He asked that I come to the lab to see him in person, since he couldn't deliver the message verbally. I would have to see the message, rather than hear it. He surprised me by asking that I not tell anyone else that he had called. I could accept that, since I had already excused myself until 7 p.m. that night, when I was to meet Rosini at the station to begin our stake-out in a battered old car he had found for the operation.

Harry was flushed and breathing heavily when I arrived at the lab. "Come in here," he whispered loudly, while he motioned to a small conference room. He had the footprint casts of footprints discovered at the murder scene and at the location near the hospital where Joanne's body had been found. He spread them out on the conference room table. To this collection, he also added the barefoot prints of the orderly, Mason. The complete report had just arrived. "You need to sit down before I share it with you," Harry cautioned, in a manner which departed from his usual calm, detached presentation. "This is going to blow your mind away, I promise." He continued, with an increasing respiratory rate and quickening speech that convinced me the report must contain something extraordinary.

"O.K., show and tell time," he said, while motioning to the casts. "I've arranged them in the order they are discussed in the report. Now, just follow it along, and don't peek at the last page. It will spoil the conclusion." I followed Harry's instructions, and methodically followed the report, while examining the casts as they were mentioned in the report. Harry paced nervously, impatiently popping his knuckles while he walked. I finally came to the last page, and he stopped abruptly behind my chair, reading over my shoulder, as though he hadn't read it before. I came to the conclusion, which had so thoroughly agitated him, and I gasped.

"See, see what I told you!" Harry nearly shouted in his excitement. "What are you going to do now?" He hopped from one foot to the other. I was exceptionally grateful that I had just spent four relatively restful days and nights away from here. I would need that fortification.

"Have you shown this report to anyone else?" I asked. Harry assured me that he had not. "Then I want you to immediately lock it in your safe, after sealing it in an envelope, on which you will write in big, bold letters, that it is your private and confidential communications, and that nobody else is to read it." He nodded, and followed my instructions. When he was finished, I continued. "Now box up those print casts, all of them, and put a similar note on them. Lock the box in your file cabinet.

"Now, I want you to keep this information just between you and me, do you understand?" He nodded. I continued, "I mean, you aren't to tell your boss or my boss, not your best friend, your psychic advisor, your priest, nobody, not a soul." He again reassured me that he would keep it a secret. I agreed to tell him my plans as soon as I had any. Of course, I lied. Instead, I called Dan for advice.

By the time I returned home I had no time for the planned nap before meeting Rosini. Nathaniel had left a message on my answering machine. As I listened to his deep, sexy voice, a florist van arrived, delivering beautiful roses in his name. When I called to thank him, I had to leave my love and thanks on his voice mail. Apparently his political supporters had planned a "Welcome Back" reception for him, to reaffirm the bright outlook for his political career. He understood I had more pressing matters to attend, and planned to attend the party alone. I sighed. The romantic reunion I had envisioned would have to be postponed. It was probably better that way, since I didn't think I had enough reserve stamina to handle the reunion and still stay awake all night on stake-out with Rosini.

Seven o'clock rolled around sooner than I expected. I didn't think I was ready, but I showed up anyway. Rosini asked me to drive while he looked at everything on the streets with night vision glasses. We cruised all night, but saw nothing, and were no closer to solving the crime the next morning than we were when we started. Of course, I didn't share with him the information locked away in Harry's safe and file cabinet. We agreed to meet at 7 p.m. again the next night, and continue with our stake-out. Again, I showed up as planned.

Rosini and I assumed the same roles we had filled the night before. I drove, while he observed. For the first part of the night it seemed that we would come up empty handed again. We stopped at a little coffee shop to fill our thermos and empty our bladders, then continued.

Around two a.m. Rosini excitedly pointed at a rag-tag figure staggering near the curb. "Pull over," he hissed, in a half-whisper. I began to protest, pointing out that this was just a harmless drunk, and we should call a squad car to come pick him up. The old Rosini, the one who had to be in control of everything and everyone, replied, "Just shut up and pull over! I don't see you solving this crime anyway, so why not see what this guy knows! Do you have some better plan, out here in the middle of the night?" I pulled over, if for no other reason than to shut him up.

Rosini got out to confront the drunk. From the appearance of his dirty, tattered clothes, it looked like he was homeless as well as drunk. Maybe he had seen something worthwhile, that would help with the investigation.

"O.K., pal, come with me," Rosini commanded, flashing his badge to the poor unfortunate man. He complied, but not before tripping and nearly falling off the curb. Rosini, reached out and helped steady the man, so he could regain the small amount of balance his inebriated mind would allow.

I heard him slur his question to Rosini, "W-What did I do, occifer?" he asked. "I ain't hurt anything, just goin' for a walk, you know."

"Just sit here with us in the car, so we can talk to you." Rosini grabbed his arm to steer him to the car, and to keep him from tripping again. In moments, he had shoved the foul smelling man into the front seat, and slid into the back seat behind him. I thought that was odd, but he seemed to have it under control. He would question the man from one angle, while keeping an eye on him, and I'd keep an eye on him from another angle. I personally didn't think the poor man needed to swivel his head around so much, and was afraid he might throw up in the car if we weren't careful. He reeked of body odor, whiskey and cigarettes. I started to roll down a window to get a breath of clean air, but Rosini stopped me. I could see no value in staying inside a closed-up car as it filled with stench, but he said again that he knew what he was doing. I decided to play along with whatever he was doing, to see what it was.

I started to take the lead with questioning the drunk, but Rosini stopped me. I expected as much, since it was his nature to want to take the lead, especially over a woman, even one who was his supervisor.

"O.K. pal, you killed a woman around here, awhile back, strangled her with a leather band, do you understand?' I tried to stop this bizarre line of questioning. This homeless drunk could not have walked out in the country to Joanne's house, then strangled her, then moved the body. I started to tell Rosini as much, but he continued. "You hid in her car in the hospital garage, didn't you, then you drove it back here, dumped her body, and took the car back to her house, didn't you?" The drunk gave him a blank, puzzled look, but said nothing.

Just as I tried to stop Rosini again, he turned on me, with a look filled with hate. "You just shut up, slut!" He'd never called me that before. Was he bucking for a demotion? Maybe he thought his little second income from the handmade hunting calls would support him if he was fired. I didn't know what was going through his mind. His eyes blazed with raw emotion. He shouted at me, "You didn't solve this crime, because you can't! You're not the hot shot detective everyone thinks you are. But old Rosini is going to solve this one, then they'll see!"

He suddenly turned to the befuddled drunk in the front seat. "You are a killer, see, and you are going to prove it. The lady cop here caught you, so you are going to kill her, with her own gun." I turned to him, stunned.

I didn't recognize his face. He had pulled his own revolver and held it to the drunk's head. "Now, take the lady's gun," he commanded. The drunk awkwardly reached out to pull my gun from its holster. Rosini had taken me by surprise. I hadn't thought to pull my own gun. This was supposed to be a routine interrogation.

"O.K., now, point it at her," Rosini commanded the drunk.

"Hey man, I don't know how to use this," the drunk told him.

"You won't have to, dummy," Rosini responded. "I'll shoot her. But nobody will know, because then, I'll have to shoot you, trying to save my partner, you see." The drunk still looked puzzled, but the answer was clear to me. Almost all of the puzzle pieces came together at once.

"Rosini, you killed her, didn't you?" I asked. "That's why your footprint appears inside one of the bigger shoes that were stolen from the orderly. The strange inner print matched your foot size exactly. So, you had planned the killing for quite some time. I just don't understand."

"Well, well, the brilliant lady detective finally figured out something!" He cackled. "Too bad you won't be alive to get the credit!"

"But why?" I asked. "She was your friend."

"You're just stalling, and I'm wise to you. But, I'll give you the answer, let's call it your dying request, shall we?" His face had taken on the distorted look of a madman.

"She was my friend. I thought I knew her, but she was a fag, you know a lesbian. When I was looking after her place, I found love letters in her cedar chest - from a woman lover. The phony. I thought she was good and pure... I knew it was useless to explain to Rosini that those letters were from one Sister to another and the love they expressed was the purest of holy loves. Only his twisted mind would distort that type of greeting. He continued his rant, "Then when I was visiting a friend at the City police station and saw that other file on the geeky kid's desk, I knew what I had to do.. It was a sign from above. I couldn't let her get away with the sham. She was evil. Do you understand?" He screamed, out of control. : She wasn't good. She wasn't a saint…"

"Like your mother?" I asked. He became more agitated than I thought possible. But before he could shake his gun at the drunk or me again, I heard the snap of handcuffs clicking shut. The drunk had miraculously sobered in a matter of a moment, and had swung around with the agility of a completely sober, trained policeman. Grabbing Rosini's hand, he snapped handcuffs on his wrist, then swiftly joined the other wrist to the shackled arm, disengaging Rosini's gun in the process.

Turning to me with a familiar, engaging smile, the drunk said, with a voice of clarity and assertiveness, "Would you like to read Mr. Rosini his rights, Detective Larsen? After all this is your case. I'm just a visitor from down south"

"Yes, I think I would like to do that," I smiled into Dan's azure blue eyes. I turned to Rosini and repeated words he had heard and said hundreds of times,

"You have the right to remain silent, Mr. Rosini. Anything you say, can and will be used against you in a court of law."

He looked like a small boy now, all of the pomp and arrogance drained from his face. Noticing that his lips were moving, I leaned closer to try and hear what he was saying. He was talking to his mother, in a little boy's voice, pleading with her to understand, "I know mamma, I need to be punished. I'm so sorry. I killed you, then I killed her. I was a bad boy. A bad boy…"

"Seems like we just said good-bye yesterday," I said to Dan.

He answered with a grin. "Yeah, just can't stay away from each other, can we? How about we get this guy checked into the jail, and talk about where we go from here, uh, after I take a bath and change clothes?" I nodded and shifted the old car into drive.

Case Closed.

Sam Larsen Mysteries

Part Two

The Aftermath - Honeymoon Homicide

PROLOGUE

Nathaniel's strong arms encircled my waist, as we clung to each other on the deck of our honeymoon cruise ship. We swayed gently to music, and he softly hummed in my ear. It seemed like we had waited for eons for this moment. Over the course of our relationship, fate threw barriers in our path every time we got close to a wedding. But it finally happened. The mesmerizing rhythm of ocean waves lapped against the ship. I had heard that sounds of ocean waves relaxed the soul, but had never paused my busy, sometimes frantic life long enough to experience it. For a few brief moments in time, I shared a love of the sea, and my heartbeat slowed to match the rhythmic swoosh, swoosh, swoosh of the waves.

In hindsight, knowing what I know now, I think the rhythmic waves were more of an omen, sloshing out a warning of things that were quickly to descend upon us.

Chapter One

Our honeymoon cruise had been as perfect as a romance novel. Even though I am not romantic by nature, I was caught up in the fairytale ambiance that pseudo- isolation from the cares of a hectic outside world offered. We had spent three days away from the world of law enforcement and court, allowing us to focus only on each other. Nathaniel was a respected judge, and I was a senior homicide detective. Our lives could only be described as hectic and unpredictable. We had waited three long years to experience a time for just the two of us. I knew before we married that I loved Nathaniel, but I was pleasantly surprised at the depth of emotions and intensity of passion such quality time brought to the surface. Our bodies melted into each other as our lips locked in a consuming kiss that made time stand still.

Our blissful world was invaded suddenly by sounds of someone stumbling towards us. I glanced in the direction of the odd erratic footsteps. I couldn't believe my eyes. A man who appeared drunk, staggered towards us, grasping his crotch. Although his gait was uneven, following a zig-zag pattern across the deck, his pace was faster than I thought possible by one so obviously inebriated. Nathaniel stepped towards the man, attempting to stop his obscene journey. He stepped between the man and me and confronted him, saying in his most authoritative judge's voice, "Hey man, you can't do that in public. Take it to your cabin if you want to fondle yourself.."

Nathaniel's diatribe abruptly ceased, and his words trailed off as the man hissed, " On fire. I'm on fire!!" He grabbed his genitals more firmly, lurched forward and fell to the deck, hitting the floor with a loud thud before either of us could catch him.

The man released the grasp on his crotch, and his hand fell limply to his side. I wondered if he had been knocked unconscious by the fall. I stooped to check his pulse. There was none. He was unresponsive and not breathing. "Go get help!" I shouted to Nathaniel. "If you see an AED hanging on the wall somewhere, grab it too." I ripped the man's shirt open and started CPR. As I performed compressions on his chest, there was no recoil. For a man who appeared to be in good physical shape, his body seemed extremely soft and limp. Although he had appeared drunk, I detected no smell of alcohol on his breath. Something made me feel uneasy about putting my mouth on his, so I continued hands only CPR for what seemed like an eternity, until Nathaniel appeared with the captain, a ship's nurse, and an AED.

I was exhausted and soaked in perspiration from the physical exertion of doing CPR without a break. I gladly stepped aside to allow the nurse to take over. She attached the AED pads to his chest and turned it on. The machine analyzed our mystery man's cardiac rhythm and announced, "no shock advised." That meant he had either regained a pulse or had flat-lined, with no shockable rhythm. I knew it was unlikely that the AED was malfunctioning. Having pushed on his flaccid chest for many minutes, I also doubted he had regained a pulse. I was correct. The nurse shook her head, indicating he had no pulse. She started an IV and prepared to administer Epinephrine as I took over CPR again.

The man looked dead. His color was blue, foamy spittle outlined his lips, and his eyelids were open. One needs muscle activity to close eyelids, and he lacked muscle tone anywhere on his body. The nurse placed an IV catheter in his vein, but she stopped short of starting IV fluids or medications. She motioned to his underside. I followed her gaze and saw the telltale signs of lividity, indicating his circulation had ceased. We both knew CPR was not going to bring him back to life.

The nurse sent a staff member to the ship's Infirmary for a stretcher and sheet. I followed as they transported the body off the deck. Something struck me as very wrong about the situation. The mystery man likely died of cardiac arrest, but I didn't think there was anything natural about his death. I whispered my apologies to Nathaniel, as I passed him on my way to the Infirmary. I invited him to join us, and he silently fell in step into the odd, macabre parade.

Chapter Two

When we arrived in the Infirmary, I identified myself to the nurse, who introduced herself as Sandy. I told her although I was a homicide detective, I had no desire to act in that capacity on the ship. I couldn't completely avoid involvement since I was a witness to the man's death, but I had no desire to disrupt my honeymoon to become embroiled in police work outside of my jurisdiction.. But the cop inside me couldn't walk away without making sure evidence was preserved. Even if it wasn't a homicide, I believed someone in the man's life would want answers to his mysterious death. I helped Sandy secure paper bags over his hands to preserve any evidence that might lurk beneath his nails, and together we performed other routine tasks to make sure if there was any evidence on the body, it would not be lost.

As we worked, I shared my gut feeling with her that the mystery man's death was suspicious. I suggested she get a blood sample before he further deteriorated, to go with his body to a medical examiner for an autopsy. I knew that some drugs and body chemistry distorted quickly after death, and felt it was important to get the sample quickly. Even though a medical examiner would draw blood at the time of autopsy, I felt it was important to get a sample before then. It might be especially informative, and I was sure it would be appreciated. She asked me to resume hands only CPR to get a little circulation started to help her draw a small blood sample. The unused IV line she had placed earlier made the task easier. Without any oxygen in it, the blood didn't look red. It was almost black, and added to the surreal death scene.

We were due to dock off the Texas coast early the next day. The captain planned to turn the body over to a medical examiner there for possible autopsy. It became a priority to identify the man, and to secure any other evidence that might exist. Sandy confided in me that it might not be that simple. A mystery illness had broken out onboard, and they were waiting for directions from the CDC on what actions to take. They were used to intestinal illnesses that sometimes break out on crowded cruise ships, but this one appeared to be respiratory and appeared to spread through the air. Sandy looked exhausted and worried. I had a feeling that the situation was much worse than she let on, and I had a premonition that my dream honeymoon had just entered into the perfect storm territory. Maybe I picked up uneasy body language from Sandy, but my gut feeling goaded me forward to gather as much evidence as possible, as soon as possible.

According to a credit card in his pocket, the deceased was John Smith. The name sounded like an alias, but it was possible that was really his name. For purposes of securing evidence, it didn't matter. We could dig deeper into his true identity once I examined his cabin. before the cleaning crew destroyed evidence. For my purposes, knowing the name he used onboard was good enough.

Without any evidence to the contrary, we spread word among the crew that the man had died of a heart attack. I discovered that death aboard a cruise ship was not uncommon. Many passengers were retirees intent on fulfilling bucket lists, who brought a bucket load of chronic health conditions on board with them. Others were unaware of fatal conditions lurking beneath seemingly healthy exteriors when they boarded their cruise. And there were the occasional suspicious deaths, traumas, and drownings. The ships were equipped with a morgue to store bodies without disrupting the cruise for other passengers. Security onboard was mostly focused on safety of the living and rudimentary preservation of evidence. But they depended on outside law enforcement to investigate suspicious deaths.

I had no doubt that gossip would spread like wildfire, so we were determined to use it to our advantage. In case it was more than a natural phenomenon, I didn't want to risk spooking a potential murderer to jump ship and disappear. There was no probable cause to stop passengers from disembarking at pre-scheduled ports of call without arousing suspicion. So no effort was made to limit exits from the ship. Our only tactic was to limit suspicion and prevent panic. Little did I know that fear of someone jumping ship would soon be moot.

The captain instructed Sandy if anyone showed up to claim or view the body, to make sure their identity was confirmed and recorded. As a safeguard against contaminating evidence, we decided there would be no viewing of the body until it was delivered to the authorities on shore.

I asked the captain to allow me access to the man's cabin. I apologized to my groom as I reluctantly gathered supplies to preserve evidence from Smith's cabin. Nathaniel gave me a good natured hug, and sealed his reassurance with a kiss. He whispered,

"I'll go back to our cabin and rest up, so I have plenty of energy for….later." He accented the last word with a lascivious wink, and left me alone to gather my gloves and plastic bags.

155

Chapter Three

The condition of Mr. Smith's cabin added to my suspicion that something was very odd in the way he died. His bed was disheveled, as though he had slept in it recently, or had entertained a sexual partner. If he had slept, it had been a restless sleep, and he had thrashed about, rumpling the sheets. There was no evidence of another person having been there. I scoured the place for evidence of another person, but found none. Using my trusty duct tape, I passed over the bedding to try and snag hairs or other miniscule evidence. I harvested one lone blond hair

I found a pair of trousers and underwear strewn on the bathroom floor, as though they had been pulled off in haste and were left where they landed. When I picked up the trousers, I noticed a large damp spot on the crotch, and wondered if he had peed his pants for some reason. I picked up the matching damp boxers and noticed a similar stain. The white fabric of the boxers provided a contrast to a brownish stain.. I surmised he had spilled coffee or tea in his lap and had rushed to his cabin to change clothes. That might explain the burning sensation he described when Nathaniel asked him to stop grabbing his crotch in public. It didn't explain why the clothing was merely damp and cold, rather that warm and soaking wet, as I would have expected if the coffee had been freshly spilled in his lap.

It also appeared that Mr. Smith had been sleeping just before stumbling on deck. He was clad in clean, dry pajamas. I had no idea why he had grabbed a credit card and placed it in his pocket as he lurched out of his cabin onto the deck.

I surmised he might have been sleepwalking, or had awakened from a nightmare. So I searched his luggage and bathroom for evidence of sleeping pills or other medication that could have caused hallucinations. I found only over- the- counter motion sickness pills and a prescription of little blue pills to help him achieve an erection.

Bagging the damp underwear and trousers and other potential evidence, I affixed my initials, date and time to establish chain of custody. The pills went in another baggie. I rolled up his bedding and secured it in a plastic laundry bag provided by the crew. I felt that the time lapse between spilling the brown liquid in his lap and when he appeared on deck complaining of being on fire, held an important clue. I had a vague *déjà vu* moment when pondering that issue but I couldn't put my finger on why it tickled long lost memories.

I returned to the Infirmary with the plastic bags and asked Sandy to ensure they were locked in a secure space, awaiting transfer to a medical examiner once we docked.. I also asked to look at the body. I didn't really want to look at Mr. Smith's genitals, but thought it was important, given his complaint of burning sensation. We lowered his pajama bottoms without disturbing our carefully preserved evidence, and noted the condition of his crotch area. It was reddened, but not blistered, as I would have expected with a second degree burn, as if from a hot liquid. If he had only suffered a first degree burn with the dark liquid spill, redness should have subsided with a short time lapse. I would have expected a much earlier complaint with either type of thermal burn. I asked Sandy if he had visited the Infirmary earlier in the day, and she denied seeing him before his cardiac arrest. My suspicions grew larger with each unanswered clue.

Sandy and I rolled Mr. Smith's body and the bags of evidence I had collected in his cabin into his resting place in the morgue cooler. Then Sandy turned to me and dropped the information bomb I had hoped not to hear. While I had been in the Smith cabin, Sandy and the captain had been on the phone with the CDC. We were not going to be permitted to disembark from the ship once we reached port until further notice. A CDC team of medical personnel were enroute to the port to board and test every passenger and crew member for the newly identified Coronavirus, similar to a years earlier SARS virus from the Middle East. It had infected a number of individuals on the mainland. It now appeared to have infected a number of passengers who could be heard coughing and gasping in the patient rooms adjoining the morgue. Sandy worried that we would run out of morgue space before docking. She had pulled heavy duty protective equipment from storage, and she and the other medical staff now wore N95 respirators. She muttered something about it being too little too late and sighed as she politely dismissed me and told me to return to my cabin and stay there until further notice. I asked to see the captain before I isolated, and she arranged for him to meet me in the morgue.

Captain appeared as worried and exhausted as Sandy. When I asked for access to security tapes from the entire cruise, he agreed. I suspected that had it been a normal situation, and he hadn't been so obviously exhausted and preoccupied, he might have declined my request. I had expected push back. When he offered none I knew that the new virus was serious. From what he and Sandy told me, they were learning new information on the run. The CDC said that although it was in the family of viruses that we had seen before, this one was new. It appeared to have come from Asia and/or Europe, and he said that Italy was in dire condition from it, already seeing many deaths and overwhelming their hospital system. Some countries, including Italy, had issued lock down orders to limit spread. He said it sounded a lot like the 1918 flu endemic which had caught the world off guard. Against that backdrop I suspected that Mr. Smith's death might be quickly dismissed as a heart attack without any opportunity to explore answers to its mysterious circumstances. Captain seemed to humor me as I told him my intent to investigate, but he didn't discourage or challenge me. He offered to cooperate as much as he could, given the circumstances.

Chapter Four

Nathaniel was asleep when I finally made it back to our cabin. He apparently was serious when he said he had planned to rest up for later. I tiptoed over to sit on the bed without waking him. I gazed at his handsome, sleeping face and was hit by a wave of emotion and gratitude that God had smiled on me so generously with such an exceptional husband. I resisted the urge to finger comb his lavish wavy head of mahogany hued hair. Equally lavish lashes framed the eyelids that hid his mesmerizing hazel eyes with their gold flecked highlights. His full lips curved naturally into a subtle smile even as he slept. His muscled body gave me a thrill, even without physical contact.

Nathaniel's attractiveness went much deeper than his physique and chiseled good looks, however. I found his kindness and natural gentle nature equally attractive. His moral compass, which governed his fairness as a judge acted as an aphrodisiac, when contrasted against the ugliness and injustice humans often perpetrated against each other. We had met when I testified in a murder trial in his court. I had transferred to Iowa from Texas after a divorce from Dan, my fellow police officer and first husband.

Dan and I were similar in temperament and were passionate people who had both loved and fought with equal passion. We had dismantled our relationship through a series of passionate disagreements that overshadowed our passionate love affair. Too often we communicated with each other in the same manner as our interrogation techniques with hardened criminals. It had not been a recipe for marital success.

The marriage had lasted two volatile years. The smoldering ember of attraction had not been entirely extinguished, however. We were drawn to each other like moths to a flame, and we had fallen into passionate trysts together even after our divorce. It was impossible to avoid each other. Our paths crossed during police work, and we somehow managed to extend the connections that began professionally to our personal lives.

I had learned a lot from my marriage to Dan, and I had worked with a counselor on issues that had destroyed my marriage to him before I considered marrying Nathaniel. I didn't want to repeat my mistakes. I knew the only way to prevent a second failed marriage was for me to take ownership of my role in the failure of my first marriage. I couldn't stop being a passionate person. Nathaniel didn't want that, and I couldn't be anyone other than who I am. But I was determined to learn how to communicate appropriately, and how to establish boundaries between work and my home life.

I had spent time in Iowa during a murder investigation that had fronts in both states. When it became obvious that Dan and I could not stay away from each other, I applied for a position in Iowa and was hired as a deputy commander of a homicide unit in the Iowa county where I had spent time investigating the Texas murder case. My experience in Texas, coupled with my degree in psychology helped earn me a promotion to commander after the unit commander retired. I hadn't been eager to enter into a new romance, so my relationship with Nathaniel had evolved slowly. We remained friends for nearly a year, enjoying each other's company and intellects without any thought to progress towards romance. It had been a very subtle transition, which surprised both of us.

Nathaniel and I had dated for years before marrying. Together we formed an attractive couple. Some in our city called us a power couple. I wasn't sure I approved of that characterization, but given Nathaniel's political aspirations and the professional respect we both earned in our careers, I understood it was a natural impression.

While Nathaniel was darkly handsome, I looked the part of my northern European heritage. I had a girl- next- door attractiveness that was more cute and wholesome than glamorous or classically beautiful. I had cropped my strawberry blond hair to a medium short bob to accommodate my busy life. My ivory pink skin freckled in the sun. The sprinkling of freckles across my nose and cheeks made me look younger than my age. It offered me an advantage when I surprised criminal suspects, who underestimated my years of experience and investigative expertise.

I shifted mental gears and mused about my life with Nathaniel. Our wedding had been an elegant, understated event. I would have been happy with a simple civil ceremony at the courthouse or an elopement to Las Vegas, but we both understood the need to seal our nuptials in a traditional ceremony that fit Nathaniel's public image and political aspirations. The stress induced weight loss I had achieved during the Cavenaugh murder trial had enabled me to fit into a sleek sheath without pre wedding dieting. We had kept our ceremony simple, with an intimate guest list. But we spent most of our budget on an all-out bash for our reception. Our 200 guests partied with us late into the night, celebrating our union with exuberance that contrasted the understated elegance of our wedding ceremony. We had rested up from wedding exhaustion at a beachside hotel before boarding our cruise ship.

Now I sat next to my new husband, saddened that our blissful isolation had been brought to an abrupt end with the intrusion of Mr. Smith and his untimely death.. I cut my musings short, stripped off my sweat soaked clothes, and slipped into a hot, steamy shower. Deep in thought, I worked the citrus scented body wash into cotton candy-like suds and stepped under the hot shower spray. I wasn't aware that the sound of my shower had wakened Nathaniel until I was suddenly enveloped by his strong, warm arms. His gentle sensual hands took over the task of soaping every surface and crevice on my weary body. My exhaustion rinsed away with the suds, and I rallied to an evening of lovemaking that blocked Mr. Smith and his mysterious burned crotch from my mind.

Chapter Five

Nathaniel did what men do after a lovemaking marathon and gave in to what biology dictated. He quickly fell into a restful slumber. I was pleasantly drowsy, but not sleepy. I curled my body next to his and let my overactive mind run away with itself. Sleep was not on my agenda, no matter how much I wanted it.

A tap on our door brought me out of my analytical musings. I grabbed a robe and answered it. James, who introduced himself as Captain's assistant apologetically smiled, averted his eyes and handed me a flash drive with the security footage that I had requested. I noticed that James wore a blue mask and kept a distance from me, standing in the hallway and quickly turned away to attend to more urgent matters. James had been tasked to discretely look at passenger records to glean what they could reveal about the life and times of our deceased Mr.

Smith. I surmised the captain would make a good investigator, since he used impressive savvy in getting the job done without arousing suspicion. He had no problem convincing the staff that he needed as much information as possible in order to notify the family. That much was true, but it wasn't the whole story. In case the death turned out to be a homicide, I wanted the investigation to land in a good jurisdiction. I hoped to glean information to help us steer the investigation in that direction. Our luck was exceptional in that regard. Mr. Smith hailed from the DFW area, squarely inside my ex-husband, Dan's jurisdiction.

I called Dan to inform him of the situation, and to ask for his help. I explained that the death appeared natural, but my detective's gut said it was far from routine or natural. I knew Dan respected my detective's instincts and skills, and if there was anyone in the world who would take my suspicions seriously, it would be him. Dan and I had solved many complex cases together. He was an excellent detective with keen investigative instincts. He agreed to help as much as he could, but informed me that the DFW area was on lockdown orders which confined people to their homes unless they worked essential jobs, like medical or law enforcement. Since the virus was new, nobody knew what to expect from the lockdown. Fortunately for law enforcement, the fear it generated acted like a natural curfew even for would- be criminals. So both Dan and I would find that we had time to fit in at least a cursory investigation of the mysterious death of one Mr. Smith.

Once the CDC arrived and began nasal swabs for viral testing it became clear that for the immediate future I would have ample time to work on the investigation, since we, too were on a lockdown and confined to our cabins. Sandy's prediction that there would be deaths from the virus proved to be true, but even she underestimated how far the virus had already spread among the crowded party crazed cruise ship environment. People had set sail to have fun, and they had unknowingly shared the virus with each other in the atmosphere spawned by that quest for fun.

I smiled to myself. I was a little worried that my involvement with a potential homicide investigation while on my honeymoon meant I needed to work on the boundaries a bit more. At the same time, I knew that I had made progress. The old Sam Larsen would have neglected her new husband and immersed herself totally in the case, forgetting that she was on her honeymoon at all. The old Sam would have felt no guilt towards allowing invasion of her private world by a case that begged her involvement.

Unfortunately, Nathaniel and I both were witnesses to Mr. Smith's demise. So no amount of resolutions could keep us completely isolated from it. I had hoped to keep my involvement to a minimum, but fate intervened in ways I could not have anticipated. We had no case and no proof of homicide. That frustrated me. With each piece of the puzzle, I was drawn deeper into the mystery. I knew it would take great effort to keep the Smith death from consuming my time and attention.

The investigation, itself would need to be conducted by phone, virtually through meeting software or Skype, which put me at a disadvantage. I was skilled at reading body language and facial expressions, but would be deprived of those elements in a new Coronavirus world.

Once the ship docked I called my boss, Chief Sutton, to let him know we were being detained on board. I also alerted him to the Smith situation. Chief had been a supportive boss. I was his first female senior detective among a cast of old school men, who thought a woman's place was in the home. Sometimes Chief had acted protective of me in a fatherly way during our years together. I didn't take it as an insult. I knew he respected me as an investigator, and his protectiveness had more to do with his generation and role as a father to his daughters, than anything else. I was secure enough in my own identity and professional status to accept it without making an issue where none need exist. I knew he wanted me to be happy, and he was a big fan of my marriage to Nathaniel. He had frequently pointed out how well our personalities complimented each other. Nathaniel was calm and objective, and his brilliant mind kept me intrigued and interested. I usually became bored with men I dated if they were not my intellectual match. Nathaniel had held my rapt attention for three years, and I expected that to continue for a lifetime.

Chapter Six

I settled in a comfy seat to review the security footage, and with nothing else to do, Nathaniel joined me. As a security measure, all passengers were photographed when they boarded. The ship's records showed Mr. Smith had boarded alone. He was seen in several security tapes with an attractive blond. It appeared the two had developed a romantic attraction to each other. The last recorded meeting between the two showed them having a midmorning coffee on the day Mr. Smith died.

The blond was dressed in a scant bikini, covered by a sarong. Mr. Smith barely kept his eyes off her, and made no effort to keep his hands to himself. At one point the blond dropped something on the floor, and when Smith bent to retrieve it, she reached into her sarong and withdrew what appeared to be a vial of clear liquid, which she quickly poured into his coffee. When Mr. Smith picked up the coffee cup to take a sip, the blond leaned forward.

She experienced a wardrobe malfunction that bared her breasts, and as he paused to enjoy the scenery, she bumped his hand, causing him to spill the coffee into his lap. Mr. Smith stood up abruptly and appeared in mild distress, as the hot coffee burned his private parts. His distress didn't appear to match the extent he suffered hours later. He left abruptly, walking briskly towards his cabin. I guessed from the damp underwear and trousers in his cabin that he had rushed to his cabin to change clothes.

I paused the recording and stared at the coffee soaked crotch of our deceased Mr. Smith. A partial answer to one puzzle piece stared at me from the screen. I wondered, had the blond intended to poison or sedate Mr. Smith? Or had she had second thoughts and acted deliberately to spill the tainted coffee in his lap instead? The mystery deepened.

The mystery blond had kept her face hidden during each of the recorded interludes with Mr. Smith. When I asked about her in a Facetime's interview with staff, none of them recognized her. So I was surprised when the captain was able to give me an identity. The blond had registered in her cabin as Mrs. Jane Smith. One staff member had told the captain he remembered the name because Mr. Smith had stopped him one evening to tell him. Mr. Smith had been a bit drunk at the time, and was more impressed at his clever attempts at humor than he should have been. He had stopped the staff member and told him how funny it was that he had fallen in love with a woman who shared his last name. Laughing hysterically, Mr. Smith had asked, " If we get married and she keeps her last name, would she hyphenate and become Mrs. Smith-Smith? "I didn't find it as amusing as Mr. Smith did, but I found it ironic and a bit suspicious. I suspected at least one of them was not a Smith. But stranger things had happened, so I couldn't rule it out.

Mr. Smith was an attorney in the DFW area, and ship's records provided a home and office address. He listed his sister in Nevada as his emergency contact, and listed his marital status as divorced. Mrs. Jane Smith listed no next of kin, and was single. She listed no work address or other contact information on her emergency information forms. Her home address was an apartment in a suburb north of Dallas. Captain told me that he had visited Mrs. Smith's cabin, but it appeared she had never been there. The cabin was in pristine condition.

Once we docked, the Medical Examiner at the nearest city took possession of Mr. Smith's body, and two more bodies of passengers who had died, probably from the mystery virus. The ship's doctor had opined in the medical record that the death appeared natural, with no suspicious circumstances. The opinion of a honeymooning detective meant nothing to the doctor, and I feared it would be insignificant to the ME as well. But I pressed my case, and he agreed to perform a limited autopsy, running the blood sample that Sandy had collected, and running a sample of the skin from the burned crotch through a limited exam. He explained that the casualties arriving from the virus took priority, since their autopsies would hopefully lend clues that would help medical professionals treat them and save lives. But, like me, he was committed to the principal that no murder should go unpunished, so he agreed to lend his assistance as best he could. In what I considered best case scenario, he listed cause of death as undetermined, at least for the time being.

Chapter Seven

Dan's fiancé, Debbie worked in one of the large, prestigious law firms in the DFW area and recognized Mr. Smith as a partner in one of the other large firms. She provided an unflattering profile for the womanizing, patronizing Mr. Smith and summed up his reputation as "a real jerk." According to office gossip, his wife had recently divorced him after his repeated affairs had come to light. He had made no effort to conceal them or to apologize for them. One of Debbie's coworkers had worked at the same firm as Mr. Smith, and had warned all of the female employees to steer clear of Mr. Smith and his firm. According to the coworker, he had a notorious ego and an even more notorious temper. His temper was exceeded only by his libido, which he brought to work and shared with any attractive female unfortunate enough to cross paths with him. He was physically attractive, but not attractive or wealthy enough to compensate for his ugly character. He caught unsuspecting new females off guard with his charm. But the charm quickly gave way to an uncomfortable hostile environment, replete with sexual innuendos and inappropriate behavior. As an attorney he was aware that his conduct violated sexual harassment laws, but as an attorney, he believed he was above the law, and capable of escaping the consequences of his behavior. That is, until he encountered the mysterious Mrs. Jane Smith.

Debbie's information about Mr. Smith added a lot of insight into his death. If he had been murdered, it was almost poetic that the perpetrator was a woman and his genitals a target. I reminded myself that his mode of death was still a mystery. I had a long list of questions to ask Mrs. Smith once she was located. Nobody had been able to locate Mrs. Smith on the ship, so it was possible that she had not returned to the ship after a shore excursion before the lock down.

The federal law enforcement community generally claims jurisdiction in cases where suspicious deaths occur on cruise ships while in international waters. The new virus changed priorities, and they had declined jurisdiction since I was the only one who believed Smith's death to be suspicious. They deferred jurisdiction to Dan, due to his proximity to Smith's last known address.

Chapter Eight

Confined to our cabin, I had plenty of time and energy to work on the Smith case if needed. The ship's crew worked extra hard to make passengers comfortable, while following CDC guidelines to limit contact. Our meals were delivered and left outside the cabin door, and empty dishes picked up without any interaction between staff and us. It seemed surreal.

The medical examiner ran the blood specimen I had asked nurse Sandy to draw. He said Mr. Smith's electrolytes were way off, and he wasn't surprised that his heart had stopped. It wasn't a normal panel for a normal heart attack. Potassium was off the charts, while calcium was so low it almost didn't register. In other words, Mr. Smith's lab values were inconsistent with life. Initially the medical examiner had planned to call the death a cardiac arrest due to an unknown medical condition, but the wonky lab results changed his mind. Forensics ran tests on Mr. Smith's clothing samples and of the skin in his genital area to examine it for chemicals. Both tested positive for hydrofluoric acid. Nothing on the ship used HF, and there was no reason it should have been on board.

I had worked my way through college as an EMT, and I remembered one patient that had called 9-1-1 complaining that he had been sleeping when he was suddenly jolted awake by a deep burning pain in his foot. We transported him to the hospital, and fortunately the E.R. doctor on call had a background in occupational medicine. He recognized the delayed response to a hydrofluoric acid exposure and was able to administer an antidote that inactivated the destructive HF molecules that were seeking calcium and eating away at that patient's bone and cartilage. That patient was employed at a microchip manufacturing plant that used HF to etch silicone microchips. He remembered spilling a small amount of HF on his foot earlier in the day. He had washed the area, but hadn't reported it or gone to the company nurse, who would have administered a calcium gluconate antidote right away. He mistakenly thought that if the acid didn't burn immediately, he must have neutralized it with the water. He had nearly lost his foot because of that mistake.

HF is relentless. It penetrates the skin and underlying tissue, and seeks calcium. In lower doses it doesn't burn right away. But it makes up for it later as it penetrates, then does its destructive work deep inside the body. It can burn skin, but its real damage is much worse, much deeper, much more deadly. An exposure the size of one's hand can cause cardiac arrest due to HF depleting the body's calcium, which is needed for muscle contraction. The heart muscle needs calcium and finely balanced electrolytes in order to contract and pump blood. While flushing an exposed site with copious amounts of water helps with other chemicals, like nitric or sulfuric acid used in the microchip manufacture process, it isn't enough for HF exposures. Those need the antidote to stop the HF molecules.

I suspected that the liquid spilled in Mr. Smith's lap had contained HF. If he had swallowed the HF laced coffee he would have quickly died an excruciating death, which would have been identified as suspicious enough for a homicide investigation. If Mrs. Smith's actions to prevent him from swallowing the liquid had been on purpose, it created more questions than answers.

While pre- meditated, it cast doubt on whether her intent had been to kill him. If she had gone to the lengths to bring HF onto the ship and to hook up with Mr. Smith, what was her purpose? My pulse raced, as it always does when I launch into a murder investigation. I was more impatient than usual. I wanted a definitive cause of death and I wanted it soon! If Mr. Smith had been murdered, evidence and witnesses, not to mention the perpetrator would quickly slip through our hands once we were allowed to go ashore.

The mystery deepened. HF was readily available in microchip manufacturing. Occupational spills or exposures happened with enough regularity in an industrial setting that company medical staff kept calcium gluconate on hand to administer right away. But an HF exposure on a cruise ship would be unexpected and not accidental. A ship's doctor and nurse would not be prepared to administer the antidote to stop the damage, even if it was available. They would have no reason to even have an antidote on hand. I had to admit, the perpetrator who exposed Mr. Smith to HF knew what she was doing, and knew he likely would suffer without appropriate medical treatment.

Spilling HF on a person while out to sea on a ship where nobody would suspect HF and be able to help the victim was darkly brilliant. The coffee likely diluted the HF enough that it didn't initially elicit a chemical burn, so Mr. Smith probably thought he had only suffered a thermal burn from the hot coffee. He had stripped off his clothes and washed the exposed area, but that was not nearly enough to stop what followed.

Chapter Nine

The blond hair I had gathered from my brief examination of Mr. Smith's room turned out to be artificial. So our mysterious Mrs. Smith wore a wig! She had apparently been careful not to leave any other biological specimens on Mr. Smith. The hair and HF were the only evidence found on Mr. Smith or his belongings.

Dan's fiancé, Debbie. was a natural asset to our investigation, given her proximity to the legal community. Dan had convinced her to help us in an unofficial capacity. She had already given us a good beginning background on Mr. Smith, but we needed to delve deeper into his past. Office grapevines often provided a wealth of information not available to officials on official missions. She had demonstrated a talent for knowing how to extract information without raising suspicions. She had deftly pried enough information from her "sources" without letting on that they were, indeed sources. She compiled a portfolio of women known to have been victimized by Mr. Smith, and had even established their whereabouts at the time of his death. The few who remained would be sorted and compared to social media posts to investigate whether they or a person in their sphere was anywhere near Smith at the time of his death.

If only we had such luck with Mrs. Smith. The North Dallas address she had provided on her cruise paperwork did not exist. She had left no financial trail, either. She had left no obvious prints in Mr. Smith's room, and the belated discovery of her spiking his coffee with the clear liquid concealed in the vial in her sarong, offered us no opportunity to find and test the coffee cup for prints. The cruise ship had been thoroughly cleaned and her cabin reassigned to isolate people who tested positive for the virus, before we had an opportunity to dust it for fingerprints or anything that would help us discern her real identity.

Once the lab tests revealed an exposure to the HF, we had a homicide ruling from the ME, and I was relieved and excited. I was more than ready to get into the race to find the killer. Dan, Debbie, and I scheduled a Skype session to strategize our investigation. Thanks to Deb's unofficial background investigation into Mr. Smith's activities, we knew that he had no current girlfriend, and had bragged to colleagues that he was going on the cruise to "hook up with as many chicks as I can." He didn't appear to be depressed over his divorce, but was noticeably restless and missing female company

Smith was a talented litigator. He was also a rain maker, bringing in lots of wealthy clients. So the Firm's managing partner and administration turned a deaf ear and blind eye to his escapades. He found himself aging and alone. Smith began showing signs of a midlife crisis. He showed no remorse for womanizing, and nobody felt sympathy for him when his wife divorced him. But he showed signs of trying to outrun Father Time. He dyed his hair and changed his hair style. He had taken a month off work to recover from laser skin tightening and liposuction to sculpt his midsection. Then there was the bright red sports car. He had become a caricature of male midlife crisis. It was no surprise that he had booked a cruise so he could cruise for fresh meat. We asked Deb to delve deeper. We needed more history. I asked for a five year look back on his life. Perhaps the elusive Mrs. Smith lurked somewhere in the shadows of his life somewhere along the timeline.

All we had to date was a photo of Mr. Smith as he appeared after death and a new one Deb had found from the legal directory at his Firm. Mr. Smith was handsome but not strikingly so. His money and power in the community made him more attractive than he was in real life. I was struck by how average he looked in death. He wasn't short, but not tall either. His hair was a dark brown. But after viewing his pubic hair during my on- board exam, it appeared his real hair was salt and pepper grey. Deb said his coworkers described his light blue eyes as steely and cold.

Ships the size of ours could hold more than 2,000 passengers plus crew. Our wedding was during off season for cruises, so the ship had booked only 1400 passengers. Even at less than capacity, with the addition of a couple hundred crew, that totaled a daunting number of potential perpetrators. We didn't know if we were dealing with one or several perps. We needed to start somewhere to begin narrowing the potential pool of suspects down to a manageable number.

Dan cleared his throat before he spoke, so I knew he was uncomfortable with what he was about to suggest. He said, "We need someone to help manage some of the technology on this case. Especially someone with good social media skills. Before you go nuts on this next suggestion, remember it is all about results, OK?" I had a sinking feeling in the pit of my stomach. The virus had turned normal resources and operations upside down, so I knew he wasn't going to recommend any regular police resource.

Those were strained in trying to proceed normally during an historically abnormal pandemic situation.

Dan continued, "I have already cleared with my department to bring on a contract person to do the kind of computer support we need. We know of one, but since you are the only one with time on your hands, we would need for you to be our liaison and his handler. We want you to approach Mr. Peales to see if he will consider hiring on temporarily for this case."

I heard a scream and realized it was me. I made a weak attempt at humor. "Was that my outside voice?" I asked. "I hadn't meant to let my inner voice out. Sorry. You know I don't like Mr. Peales. He gets on my nerves. I know he did a good job on the social media investigation that helped us solve the Cavanagh case, even though he wasn't supposed to." I begrudgingly admired his proficiency and talent with the computer and social media. I also remembered he had almost ruined the investigation when he went rogue in his efforts.

I was busy rolling my eyes when Dan reminded me I was on screen and they could see my every move and expression. I didn't apologize. I stuck out my tongue just to show how juvenile I could be and how little I cared that I was acting like a child. Deb spoke up. Even her rebuke was grown up and gentle.

"Sam, I don't know if you are aware, but Danny Peales just found out he has Asperger's, a mild condition that is part of the autism spectrum. He posted it on his Facebook last month." I put my eyes and tongue back where they belonged. I was ashamed enough of my behavior that I didn't ask why she was keeping up with Mr. Peales on Facebook. It didn't matter, anyway. Deb volunteered the answer before I asked the question. When Dan mentioned Peales' contributions to the Cavenaugh case, Deb had checked him out on Facebook to see if he was working. She had sent him a Friend request, and even though he didn't know her, he had accepted it. He was such a naïve kid. I felt squeamish at the thought of him working on the case with us.

Mr. Peales' social awkwardness suddenly made sense. It was no mystery that he was close to genius when it came to technology. He had not used good sense or judgment in using his skills, and had gained my ire because of it. No doubt he would need someone to closely supervise him to make sure he didn't blow the investigation because he couldn't appropriately interact with people online or in person without some guidance. I reluctantly agreed to be that person.

Mr. Peales' social awkwardness due to his autism didn't explain his poor personal hygiene that I detested so much, though. I learned that many with Aspergers are actually compulsive, and germaphobes, themselves. I thought that Mr. Peales would have been a more palatable encounter if he had been a compulsive hand washer. But he was not. He seemed to have a nonstop supply of mucous streaming from his nose. He didn't use a Kleenex without being prompted, and he didn't wash his hands after blowing his nose. I found that disgusting. But with infection control measures being implemented because of the new virus, maybe someone else would take the role of hygiene police with him. I was relieved that my interaction with him would be on screen or on phone only.

I can't stand it when little kids walk around with snot bubbles coming out their nose. I want to give their parents a Kleenex, and tell them to stop walking around oblivious to their kids' germy condition. I wondered if Mr. Peales' mother had been one of those oblivious parents, and that was why he had grown up with so little awareness of manners and hygiene.

Dan apparently forgot he was on screen and visible to me. I noticed a smirk that told me he remembered how much I detested poor hygiene. He shared his memories with Deb, so she wouldn't think we were withholding important private jokes from her. He recounted how I had once told a complete stranger at the movie theater to go wash his hands. It had been a spontaneous outburst on my part. I was in line at the concession stand when the man had gone into the bathroom. He came out again very quickly, and I guessed he hadn't taken time to wash his hands. So, again using my outside voice when my inside voice was talking, I had asked him if he had remembered to wash his hands. After all, he was getting ready to stand in line to get food. The vision of his germy hands touching anything that touched food had turned my stomach. So I asked him. He had looked surprised, and mumbled an apology to me before ducking back into the bathroom to wash his hands. Dan had been equally shocked and embarrassed. But other customers in the concession line had actually applauded me.

During my past encounters with Mr. Peales and his lack of hygiene, I had likewise ordered him to wash his hands. I had no intention of being easy on him this time, especially with the pandemic, which made good hygiene essential. I hoped to solve the case before it became necessary to interface with Peales in person. He was supposed to be locked down, along with all other non -essential workers, so that plus the geographic distance gave me a temporary reprieve.

I was more than a little apprehensive about bringing Peales in on the Smith murder investigation. My experience with him on the Cavenaugh case had been less than positive. The fact that he had Asperger's explained his behavior, but also gave me more cause for concern. I had noticed an extra measure of innocence in his interactions with others during the Cavenaugh investigation. While he was brilliant with social media, he was obsessed with it to the extreme. I theorized he was so obsessed with social media because he was so socially awkward and the social network friends who he had never met in person were his real friends. He also had no filter and seemed to lack common sense. He lacked the ability to read and interpret facial expressions or body language. So what he read on social media posts became his reality. It was literal, one dimensional and impersonal. But it was his reality and comfort zone.

I was afraid he would tip our hand on the investigation if we tried to use him to link to potential suspects via Facebook. On one hand it was refreshing to meet someone who didn't seem to be able to lie. On the other hand, he seemed to lack discretion, and that concerned me.

I decided before I approached Peales that I should research Asperger's syndrome so I would better understand what I was dealing with and how to better handle him. I had experienced firsthand how he took everything literally. I realized I would need to exercise caution in communicating with him. I tended to use irony and sarcasm a lot and would need to eliminate anything subtle or ironic when communicating with him. Not only would he not understand it, he would undoubtedly misinterpret it, and it would be potentially disastrous if he acted on a communication short circuit. What I had perceived as disregard for authority or instructions in the Cavenaugh case had actually been due to his inability to interpret my communication, coupled with his singular focus on the object of his obsession. I couldn't afford to make such a mistake in the Smith case.

Chapter Ten

I was lucky that our honeymoon cabin was luxurious and well positioned on the ship. It allowed us to sit on our balcony and avoid claustrophobia from being confined to a small inner cabin. I planned to spend as much time on the balcony as possible. As I soaked in the sunlight, I envisioned the ultraviolet light as a purifying element. I carried my steaming hot takeout dinner to my cabin balcony and settled in for a night's work. I pulled out my laptop and accessed the Smith autopsy file that Dan had forwarded to me earlier in the day.

The autopsy exam had been more detailed than the ME had originally planned. Once the HF had been identified, he expanded his planned exam and produced an extensive and detailed report. Mr. Smith had mild blockage of two cardiac arteries, but that hadn't contributed to his death. Had he not died from HF exposure, he likely would have had several years before he experienced any symptoms from his heart. Not so with his liver. It showed a long history of heavy drinking, and showed signs of moderate cirrhosis. The liver is a marvelous organ, however, and can regenerate damaged cells which could slow down full blown liver failure for several months or years.

Smith's body had aged beyond his biological age of mid 40's, likely due to his life style. But he fought valiantly to fix the outer façade in order to appear younger. He had hair plugs, a chin implant, and not a surprise – a penis implant to enlarge his favorite body part. I was not surprised at Deb's information harvest, which had unearthed his online dating profile and web page under the name of "Daddy Long Leg." I fought mild nausea as I read his site, and I found it hard to imagine being romantically intrigued by his postings. He failed to understand that women usually were attracted to men of genuine character and substance, and not merely genitals. His online postings were as self- consumed as his reputation in the legal community.

More disturbing were the revelations by women who had been sexually harassed and molested by him. As word spread of his death, the women seemed to come out of the woodwork, revealing not only his self-absorbed narcissism, but a blatant sexual predator who had gotten by with unspeakable acts against them for years. Many of the women had worked in the same office or in offices of his co-counsel, and had been afraid to come forward while he was alive. He had ruined more than one woman's professional reputation and chances of gaining employment in the legal community, when she had dared to report him or consult with the firm's Human Resources department after being sexually harassed.

Mr. Smith had been a real rain maker for the firm, snagging high dollar clients. So, the firm had turned a blind eye to his behavior as it pocketed the money he brought in. Many of the clients had sought his advice on how to avoid consequences of their own sexual harassment and discrimination towards their own employees. His reputation preceded him in the legal and client community, and he had profited from his despicable behavior.

The social media reports were loaded with expletives and vitriol, as his victims united online and celebrated Smith's demise. I was more than a little concerned that Mr. Peales would be permanently damaged by them. I was pleasantly surprised that he seemed unaffected, and completely absorbed with the technology tasks, apparently paying no attention to the personal comments and the slog of skin crawling filth on Smith's sites.

I begrudgingly admitted that Peales was an asset. He cross referenced the list of women that Deb had compiled against cruise manifests and social media posts. He went beyond Deb's list, with my blessing, and compiled an additional list of all women who posted on Smith's social media or made reference to him on theirs. Although extensive and comprehensive, the research brought us no closer to identifying our mystery woman, who I was almost certain was his murderer. It was the pinnacle of frustration for me to know with such certainty who the murderer was, but unable to find her or her true identity. I blamed the novel model of investigation that we were forced to use during lock down, while giving kudos to the woman who pulled off what could be viewed as a perfect crime. I was optimistic that we could have solved the case quickly, given what we knew, if we had been able to utilize our old fashioned "pre- pandemic" boots on the ground, in person investigative methods. But I wasn't ready to throw in the towel.

Knowing that HF had limited uses in industry, I asked Peales to pull together a list of all certified occupational nurses in the country. The profession is one of the smaller specialties, with a unique skills set, which includes treating on the job chemical exposures. I also asked Dan to obtain a list of occupational nurses at the handful of computer chip manufacturers in the area. Mr. Smith's close proximity to those companies gave us a starting point. In the outside chance that the mysterious Ms. Smith was really a Smith and not an alias, it offered us an opportunity for Peales to work his cross checking magic on the computer. I felt like we were so close, but yet so far away from finding our killer. It is a rare case, indeed, where I feel outwitted by a perpetrator, but this one was getting dangerously close to it.

During my years as an investigator I had investigated a case where I despised the perpetrator, but managed to detach emotionally in order to deliver an unbiased, evidence- based investigation. I sometimes disliked the victim, and many times found no reason to respect either the perp or victim. But I had never worked a case where I felt such disdain and repulsion for the victim. I usually rallied enthusiasm for a case by identifying an altruistic purpose, such as giving the victim's family a sense of closure.

When I contacted Smith's listed next of kin to deliver the death notification, she was ambivalent about finding Smith's killer. Smith's behavior alienated even his blood kin, and they had been estranged for many years. She refused to have anything to do with disposing of his remains, or in assisting me with my investigation. I left follow up contact about his disposition to the ME, who had his hands full with figuring out the same for the ever mounting number of corpses that inundated the morgue from the virus deaths. Some jurisdictions, including his, had moved refrigerated trucks in to store the overflow of bodies from the morgue. Mr. Smith's disposition would likely have to wait, and nobody seemed upset by that.

Regardless of the individuals or circumstances, I had never lost sight of my belief in justice and the legal system. I knew it had its flaws, but I never once doubted I was doing the right thing to bring a criminal to justice. I engaged in a lot of self-talk, reminding myself of that as I read Mr. Smith's autopsy. I doubted I would ever find a case like his, where I felt no sense of justice in helping to pursue whoever had killed him. I knew I would need to remind myself regularly that the person who killed Smith was the criminal, even though he, too had been a criminal for many years. He had just never been brought to justice because the victims had feared having their lives ruined further if they complained.

At the end of the day, I knew the heart of a cop, dedicated to uphold the law, still beat strongly within my being. I couldn't muster enthusiasm for the Smith case for my usual reasons. But I propelled myself forward with undiminished resolve, fueled by an investigator's innate curiosity and the deepening intellectual challenge posed by his murder. I couldn't look away and allow the murderer to avoid consequences of his or her actions. If I opened that door on the Smith case, where would it end? Would I avoid finding other murderers in the future if the victim was scum? I had taken an oath to uphold the law, wherever that journey took me. I couldn't afford the luxury of cherry picking which cases to aggressively investigate, and which ones to let slide. My self-lecture worked. I trod on with the investigation the best I could, given our logistic, pandemic related restraints.

I spent the rest of my evening reviewing the autopsy report with extreme detail, and forced myself to read his "Daddy Long Leg" postings with the same detail. I knew somewhere within those vile postings there might lurk an important clue. I couldn't afford to be distracted by his nasty rhetoric or my repulsion to it. It was almost a miracle, given the ugliness I encountered in my job, that I could have a normal love life. I smiled as I thought of my very normal, desirable husband and vowed to respond normally to him with all the passion of a newlywed for as long as we both lived.

Chapter Eleven

After reviewing the autopsy report I toyed with the idea of asking nurse Sandy for her insight, but given the strain of the virus, which was now a global pandemic, I thought better of the idea. I hadn't spent much time with her, but during our short interaction I had grown to respect her professional qualifications, and admired her strong and confident personality.

Sandy was a redhead. I wasn't sure if it was by birth or by chemical intervention, but it suited her. I thought it fit her personality to a T. She had been an ER nurse before casting her fortunes to the sea. She had initially expected life of a cruise ship nurse would be one long vacation, punctuated by mundane and routine clinic work, doling out seasickness prevention meds and aspirin. Instead she discovered the position to be challenging and interesting, and once the virus boarded her ship, it was exhausting as well. She normally worked in six month stints, 12 hour shifts on, 12 off, and also on call for emergencies during her off hours. Those shifts expanded like overstretched rubber bands once the virus boarded. Crew members who tested positive were either quarantined in makeshift isolation quarters or ended up in her infirmary to be stabilized before helicopter rides to a nearby critical care unit.

I knew Sandy's spunk and professional expertise sustained her, but suspected she was as stretched and overwhelmed as the rest of the crew. Once my two week quarantine was over and Nathaniel and I were allowed to leave, I wanted to stop by the clinic and tell her goodbye, or exchange contact information. But we weren't allowed that luxury. The fear of contagion that was especially concentrated in the Infirmary, made it off limits to any except essential medical personnel. I felt a moment of regret. As a lifelong introvert, I didn't make a lot of friends, and I wasn't usually interested in expanding my small circle of trusted friends. But I had sensed that Sandy might have been a welcome addition to that circle under normal circumstances. I respect intelligent, independent women who aren't afraid to take charge of a situation when necessary. She was all of the above.

I found myself at an impasse on my investigation. I had agreed to contact Mr. Smith's ex-wife with the death notification, and had been met with anger and indifference at his death. Before abruptly hanging up on me, the ex Mrs. Smith had told me in a spontaneous rant, in rather explicit terms how happy she was that he had met his end. She said she knew of many people who would share her celebratory response, but knew of nobody who had the guts to engineer his death. She was merely grateful to whoever had accomplished it, and felt the world was a safer, kinder place without him in it.

I spent my remaining days on board enjoying my new husband, aware that our lives together were beginning in an odd and historically unique way. We learned that while I would investigate homicides virtually when possible, I would still be on the frontlines, interfacing with the public. The Courts had quickly devised a process for virtual hearings, so Nathaniel would hold court from his home office. The Smith homicide threatened to become cold, and I knew I would be hard pressed to give it priority once we resumed our normal lives.

Once our 14 day quarantine was over, we once again had long swabs jammed into the deepest recesses of our noses, and awaited our results. If they were normal, we were allowed to disembark. We were given masks and instructions not to touch our faces, and told to observe excellent hand hygiene. I was happy about that! It was a germaphobe's dream in a surreal way. I made one last call to Captain to thank him for the herculean efforts of his crew to make our stay as good as possible. I asked him to give Sandy my contact information. I was stunned and saddened to learn that Sandy had been one of the patients who had been airlifted to a nearby hospital. She was clinging to life in an ICU, connected to a ventilator and undergoing daily kidney dialysis. It didn't seem to be a disease like any I had seen before. I worried for her and hoped she would survive.

Chapter Twelve

The scene that greeted us on shore reminded me of that fateful 9/11 day when life changed for all of us, and normal, day to day activities came to a halt as our country struggled to cope with an unimaginable tragedy. Airports were ghost towns, and airplanes sat idle on the tarmacs. By some miracle, Nathaniel and I found a car to rent, and we embarked on the very long drive north. Finding a gas station or restaurant that was open was challenging, and more than once we feared that we would run out of gas before arriving in Iowa. When we found a fast food restaurant that was open for drive through service, we stocked up as much as possible to cover our next meal and replenish drinks. To this day, I hold the food service workers in highest esteem. If anyone doubts that they were "essential," then they never needed to find food on a long, deserted road trip during a pandemic. Things we normally took for granted, like finding a public restroom that was open, became a challenge. It seemed as though we had descended into a twilight zone. I guessed it was covered by our wedding vow to love and support each other through better or for worse.

My first day at the office was equally as bizarre. Only a skeleton crew kept the office open. They were stationed at socially appropriate distances and wore masks. The lunchroom was dark and abandoned. Everyone brought a lunch that was stored and eaten at their desk. Mail had piled up in the mailroom, so I decided to lend a hand and sort it. Midway down the stack of mail I found a letter addressed to me.

I tore the envelope open. As I read it, I felt as though I had been punched in the gut by an invisible fist. It was a letter from Sandy, sent by the Captain after her death. She had left it at the Infirmary as her condition worsened, before her helicopter evacuation to the hospital, with instructions it to send to me if she didn't survive. I was deeply saddened to learn of her death, but even sadder as I read the letter.

Detective Sam, let me say it was a pleasure meeting you. I don't want you to go through your career not knowing the truth about Mr. Smith's death. I think you are the kind of detective, that it would bother you, even though you know by now that he was scum of the earth.

I am the mysterious blond Mrs. Smith, that no doubt you are looking for. I am happily responsible for taking him out of this world. I have no regrets. He destroyed my family. My sister was one of his conquests, who thought she loved him, and mistook his advances as genuine interest in her, as a person. When he dumped her and black listed her in the legal community, she couldn't get another job, so she took a minimum wage job and started drinking. She never got over her humiliation, and the last time I saw her, the once beautiful girl was an aged, defeated, addict. She eventually died of an overdose. My parents never recovered.

It was no coincidence that I was on the same cruise ship as Smith. I "Facebook- stalked" him for years, waiting for an opportunity, and when I discovered that he was booked on this ship, I arranged a temporary assignment on it. I booked a cabin under my alias, but never slept there. I remained in the crew cabin block to avoid suspicion. You see, this was meticulously pre-meditated. It is no reflection on you, that you didn't find my identity until now. You didn't fail. I just had more time, better circumstances, and a greater motive to plan the whole thing.

And me? Well, I am not as I seem on the surface, either. You see, I was born Jason, but always in my inner self felt I was Sandy. I got my nursing degree and made good money, and eventually went to another country for a sex reassignment operation. I am happy as Sandy. It is who I am. I was such a disappointment for my parents that I haven't seen them for years. It was their decision, which became mine. But they saw it as an unforgivable sin against God and them.

Two years ago I was diagnosed with breast cancer. It was the type that was made worse by Estrogen, and my oncologist told me I needed a mastectomy .I refused. In case you were puzzled by no fingerprints, you can blame my initial chemotherapy regimen, which strangely took my fingerprints away.

My oncologist wanted me to go off my Estrogen pills. I let him think that I had, but I used my cruise ship job to help me get the pills from other countries. Doctors who I worked with on the ship wrote the prescription for me, unaware that it was not just a routine prescription for a post- hysterectomy woman.

I have chosen to live and die as Sandy. After my initial infusions of chemo, after the cancer spread, I transitioned to an oral chemotherapy drug to slow down the cancer's progression. But it suppressed my immune system, and my cancer made me extra risky for infections and illnesses like the new Coronavirus. When I started having symptoms I knew I might die, and I was ready. Killing Smith was the last item on my bucket list. I have lived a great life, full of adventure and life on my terms. I wish you and I could have been friends, but fate has had a different idea. So, Detective, here's where I bid my goodbye, and I hope you stay safe from this virus.

I folded the letter and called Dan.

Case closed.

9 798889 389770 8